KISS TODAY GOODBYE

Bernie is worried — a man seems to be stalking her, and then she finds a blue-eyed man prowling around. But when she reports all this to the police, they don't seem to take her complaint seriously. The next day, whilst out walking with the dog on the moors, Bernie falls and twists her ankle. To her surprise, her blue-eyed prowler comes to her aid. He takes her home, calls the doctor and then leaves. But who is this man? She finds him very attractive, but can she trust him?

Books by June Gadsby
in the Linford Romance Library:

PRECIOUS LOVE

JUNE GADSBY

◆

KISS TODAY GOODBYE

Complete and Unabridged

LINFORD
Leicester

First published in Great Britain

First Linford Edition
published 2003

British Library CIP Data

Gadsby, June
    Kiss today goodbye.—Large print ed.—
Linford romance library
    1. Love stories
    2. Large type books
    I. Title
    823.9'2 [F]

    ISBN 0–7089–4857–X

Published by
F. A. Thorpe (Publishing)
Anstey, Leicestershire

Set by Words & Graphics Ltd.
Anstey, Leicestershire
Printed and bound in Great Britain by
T. J. International Ltd., Padstow, Cornwall

This book is printed on acid-free paper

1

'I am not neurotic!' she exclaimed directly to the burly desk sergeant, leaning on one elbow, finger poised over the keyboard of his computer.

With one eyebrow raised, he regarded her as if he had heard it all before, which, unfortunately, he had. This was the second time in a month she had been into the police station to complain about men following her and lurking about her place. Granted, she was flustered, red-faced, out of breath and, yes, a little scared. And maybe she was becoming a touch on the neurotic side, but that was understandable in the circumstances. Any woman who lived alone would feel the same, especially if, like she did, they lived in an isolated house on the fringe of the Northumberland moors.

'Aren't you that television woman?'

The sergeant narrowed his eyes and scratched behind his ear, recognition dawning.

'You know, the one who does all that fancy cooking and stuff? What's her name, again? I keep forgetting but my wife talks about her all the time.'

'Belinda Brooks, and no, that's not me.'

The eyes of the law scrutinised her more closely.

'You sure?'

'Of course I'm sure. Belinda Brooks is my sister. We're very alike, but I'm afraid I'm not much good at cooking.'

'And your name would be?'

Without waiting for her reply, he turned back to the computer and rattled a few keys.

'Yes, Bernadette Brooks. I wasn't on duty that day, but my colleague made the same mistake as I did. Got all excited thinking you were a celebrity.'

Bernie slapped the palm of her hand down on the counter in exasperation.

'Yes, and he was just as rude!'

'Now, now, miss! Let's keep calm, shall we? No offence meant, but we do get a lot of ladies your age coming in here with complaints of stalkers. You seen the fellow again, have you? The first one you complained about?'

Bernie felt a growl stir in her tightened throat. Her back teeth clenched. Remembering where she was, she thought it prudent to hold on to that short fuse of hers. She drew in a deep breath and pulled herself up to her full height, which wasn't all that high, being only five feet three.

With infinite patience she related yet again the story of the man who had followed her around for at least a week. It had happened at the end of August. It was now mid-September and although the second man in question didn't actually seem to be following her exactly, he was there on too many occasions for it to be pure coincidence.

The sergeant gave a sigh of resignation, adjusted his position on his swivel chair and placed his hands on the computer keyboard.

'All right, miss, just give me the details. The lads will check it out. Now, what did this second stalker look like?'

'Not a stalker this time, sergeant, a prowler.'

The man, whoever, whatever, seemed to be there at her every turn. She had even seen him hovering about the dark, country lane that ran from her garden to the river. He had been watching the house, she was sure of that. She had even seen him making notes on one occasion.

He was tall, broad-shouldered and had an athletic build, she told the sergeant, who rattled away busily at his keyboard, glancing up occasionally at the changing monitor screen. Age? Middle to late thirties perhaps. He was also ridiculously good-looking, though she kept this fact to herself, since it would only confirm the overweight policeman's mistaken opinion of her, thirty years of age, unmarried, unemployed, lives alone. A classic case of loneliness mingled with romantic frustrations.

Despite it being a modern world, all grown-up and free-thinking, labels were still handed out to this effect by a good percentage of the public at large who still expected one to conform to old-fashioned rules in order to be normal.

Bernie sighed. What did they know about anything? Age was something you couldn't change. It kept on coming, year after year. But the rest? Well, she was unmarried because she chose to be so, lived alone because she liked it, and was certainly not romantically inclined at present. So there!

Liar!

'He had bright blue eyes,' she remembered, then felt her cheeks grow hot when the policeman's mouth twitched into the hint of a knowing smile.

'I turned the corner and literally

bounced off him, so I was close enough to see him properly. Well, his eyes, anyway.'

In fact, he had the most remarkable blue eyes she had ever come across, fringed with long dark lashes; a straight, narrow nose above what could only be described as a firm mouth. In fact, his whole face might have been chiselled from stone. He was handsome, but with some mature lines that gave him character.

There was an impatient yelp from the floor. Bernie bent and picked up the Yorkshire terrier at her feet, looking plaintively at her. Candy was impatient to leave, and so was she.

'Cute little dog!'

'She's my mother's actually,' Bernie told the sergeant quickly.

It wasn't exactly a lie. Bernie had bought the dog for her mother last Christmas, but Rose wasn't much of an animal lover and after a week she had claimed she just couldn't cope with such an active puppy who messed up her pristine home.

'They're good company.'

The policeman reached over and allowed the dog to lick his fingers. The tiny pink tongue flicked in and out with great excitement.

'Friendly little thing, isn't she?'

Outside in the street, the autumn sun was hanging low in a turquoise blue sky with pink-tinged clouds. Bernie squinted in the strong light, set the little dog on its feet and was instantly pulled along. Candy had scented something she found just too exciting to miss.

'Oh, I'm sorry!'

The words were out before Bernie realised whom she had bumped into on rounding the corner. Candy was frantically yelping and bouncing up and down on all fours, becoming entwined with the lead of another dog. It wasn't just another dog, but another Yorkshire terrier! A male, probably slightly older than Candy and rather scruffy-looking — unlike his owner.

Steely hands gripped Bernie's upper

arms, pushing her away from his broad, muscular chest. A pair of the bluest eyes ever stared down at her in disbelief. It was him, the lurker! And this was the same corner at which she had bumped into him a few days ago.

'You really should look where you're going,' he said.

He had a deep, attractive voice with just the touch of a lilting accent tucked away somewhere belonging either to Ireland or Scotland. She wasn't sure which.

'The sun blinded me,' she defended herself sharply, then looked just as sharply away from those penetrating eyes.

She yanked hard on poor Candy's lead, which did absolutely nothing to bring the dog to heel.

'Candy, come away!'

'If she's in season I should haul her in pretty quickly. Mop here's an absolute bomb when it comes to the ladies.'

Scottish! He was definitely Scottish.

'Would you please get your dog under control!'

Bernie scowled up at him. It seemed a long way up. He was even taller than she'd thought. She yanked again on Candy's lead and the dog made a coughing, choking sound, which made her feel guilty. She hadn't meant to hurt the poor little thing.

'Now look what you've made me do!'

'I have that effect on the ladies, too,' the blue-eyed stranger said with a grin and a mischievous twinkle. 'Mop and I, we make a good team, don't we, old fellow?'

He bent down, disentangled the two dogs and picked Mop up in his arms. The dog settled down and snuggled against his master. Bernie noticed how the man's hands were large and long-fingered, and seemed to know just exactly how to caress his canine companion to soothe it.

'Thank you!' she said abruptly. 'Now, perhaps you can explain to me why you're following me about!'

The man frowned and his grin faded into a tight, lop-sided smile as he shook his head slowly.

'I don't know what you mean. We've never met.'

'Exactly! So why should you be following me?'

'I think you must be mistaken.'

'You're always there! And this is the second time you've almost bowled me over in a week!'

'Oh, that was you, was it?'

'You know very well it was me. You didn't have that dog then. Is that another ploy perhaps? I can't see it being a coincidence. You're far more a Doberman type. Now, what's your game?'

'Believe me, I'm quite innocent. Had I not been in such a hurry the other day I would have stopped and shown you just how charming I can be. Following pretty young women isn't the kind of thing I do. I prefer to tackle them head on rather than come up from behind.'

Bernie blew out a disbelieving snort

of air through flared nostrils and tried not to dwell on the fact that he had described her as pretty.

'Well, you've just done that and I can't say I care much for your approach. Now, would you please stop doing whatever it is you're doing and leave me alone?'

The grin was back, giving him a boyish look, the kind that was guaranteed to appeal to the whole female world population except those most difficult to please. It struck a frightening chord that made Bernie's heart leap ridiculously, and she hated herself for such an involuntary reaction. After all, she was decidedly off men. She had sworn some time ago that she would have nothing more to do with them. She'd been hurt enough for one lifetime, first by her father, then by Philip who had taken her life and squeezed all emotion from it during too many wasted years.

'Come on, Candy!' she snapped.

Recognising with regret that playtime

was over, the dog marched obediently by her side as they made their way down the street towards the carpark.

'Nice meeting you, too!' she heard his sarcastic remark, but refused to look over her shoulder.

'You didn't have to make such a fuss over his silly dog!' Bernie muttered out of the side of her mouth as she opened her car door and stood back for Candy to get in. 'And don't look at me like that! He wasn't your type. Far too scruffy.'

She climbed behind the wheel and fumbled with the ignition, which was proving awkward and refusing to start. Maybe it had something to do with her jangled nerves. Her hands were still trembling from the encounter with her blue-eyed prowler.

At last the engine coughed and spluttered into life. She moved forward with a jerking, kangaroo hop, stalled and had to restart all over again. That was when she looked in her mirror and saw him standing across the road,

12

complete with the tousled Yorkshire terrier and a newspaper he was pretending to read.

I've a good mind to go back to the police station, she thought, then ruled that out as being out of the question. It would make her look doubly stupid. She gave him another glance, only to find that he was no longer there. There was no sign of him walking down the street, so he must have doubled back around that infamous corner where he had almost mown her down.

A sharp tap on the window at her side made her jump. Without thinking, she wound it down and her heart started pumping at an uncomfortably fast rate as the now familiar face with the startling blue eyes came down to exactly her level.

'You seem to have a problem.'

He smiled and it was a ridiculously devastating smile that she received like a blow to her midriff.

'Need any help?'

'No! There's absolutely nothing wrong.

Thank you very much.'

She closed the window so fast he had to back off before she caught him with it.

Oh, do go away, please! I just can't cope with all this. Not today, of all days, she said inwardly.

It hadn't exactly been the best day of her life. She had awakened to one birthday card to celebrate her thirty years, from her mother, of course. Her sister, Belinda, always forgot, or was too busy doing television commercials or cooking demonstrations for women's clubs. The other mail had consisted of bills, which she wasn't sure how she was going to pay. Then the Job Centre had shaken its head sadly, again.

This had precipitated her decision to put her house on the market. Only desperation had finally dragged her feet over the threshold of the local estate agent's office. The clerk there had tried to look enthusiastic, but she knew what he was thinking. Who was going to buy a huge, old manor house, miles from anywhere, in a state of definite dilapidation? It didn't matter that she loved the place. People these days were more interested in something smaller and more modern.

Bernie gave a shaky sigh of relief as the engine fired at last and she drove away with a slight screech of tyres. She didn't even look to see if he was still there. She drove slowly and badly till she regained control of her nerves.

Yet another symptom of paranoia, she told herself with a silly, lip-wobbling smile into her rear-view mirror. If this had been thirty or forty years ago, she mused, she would have been labelled as an old-maid with a lapdog and people would assume that she was a frustrated spinster.

Well, I'm not, thank goodness, she thought. Then she thought about it again and gave a shudder of revulsion. She wasn't far removed from that old-fashioned status. She didn't even have a boyfriend any more, casual or otherwise. She had practically lived

with Philip in an off-and-on relationship for six years, more off than on,
now she came to think about it. She
had been fool enough to think that he
was serious when he promised marriage, then had believed all his feeble
excuses for backing out. In fact, she had
been something of a saint to tolerate
him, until he'd put an end to their
relationship, two years ago. Actually, it
was one year, ten months and thirteen
days, but who was counting?

Had she really been a saint? Now
that she could look back with a cool
head and a calm heart, she knew that
the saint title was far from merited.
Fool was far more appropriate. How
easy it was to see one's mistakes in
retrospect. Well, good riddance! She
hadn't known Philip was married at
first. Philip had swept her off her feet
from the very first moment she started
working as his secretary in his archi-
tects' firm.

He was rich, he was handsome, and a
universal charmer. The trouble was, he

spread his charms about, as she was to find out, and the final blow had come in the shape of a wife and family who had and always would have, first claim on him.

Used! That's what you were, Bernie Brooks! Just like your dad used your mum. When he exhausted his interest in you, he discarded you.

'Men!'

Bernie spat the single word out loudly and with enough venom to make little Candy bark and regard her with dark full-moon eyes, wondering if it was something she had done.

'Sorry, sweetheart, but we girls have got to stick together, eh? No more running off and getting involved with shady characters.'

As she came to the crossroads, she signalled left and glanced in her rear-view mirror. Behind her, a long, sleek saloon was drawing closer, then suddenly it dropped back. Bernie's stomach flipped and her foot slipped off the clutch. She was almost one hundred per cent certain that the driver was her blue-eyed lurker. She clumsily man-oeuvred to the left and drove off as quickly as she dared. She was relieved that the other car did not follow her, but went straight on.

Twenty minutes later, her headlights shedding pale, ghostly light on the darkening hedgerows, Bernie turned into the broad, sweeping drive that fronted her old, Victorian manor house. Her tyres crunched to a halt on the gravel. She turned off the ignition and sat for a few seconds, breathing deeply and telling herself she was all kinds of a fool. There had been too much anxiety in her life recently. She was ready to imagine just about anything.

But, oh, if only imagination could wave a magic wand and turn dreams into reality. She would imagine that it was not necessary to sell this beloved mansion that she had inherited from her cousin, George, eighteen months ago. She would imagine that she no longer had to suffer the indignation of being one of the many unemployed in the country. And she might even imagine that she was completely wrong about Mister Blue Eyes, who would really be nice and not someone to run away from. After all, on the surface he did look like every girl's dream.

As she got out of the car she was startled by the sound of an engine. She turned to see car headlights sweeping up the lane. She held her breath. Nobody ever came up here unless they were lost. The lane led nowhere. A few hundred yards past her house it came to an abrupt end, turned into an ancient, deep-rutted cart track, and petered out at the edge of the moors.

The only other house for miles around was the cottage just across the road from her drive. It had been empty for years and was practically derelict. It was part of her property, but since she couldn't afford the upkeep of the main house, there was little hope of ever doing anything with the cottage.

The approaching car slid to a halt

before it reached her gates. Bernie waited with wide, unblinking eyes. Her heart gave a double beat, then thumped uncomfortably in her chest. She waited for what seemed a long time, then swallowed back her fear when she heard the vehicle being backed down the lane.

It was just some lost traveller after all, who had taken the wrong turning.

2

The next day the sun shone defiantly through a network of thick white clouds scudding across a blue, windswept sky. There was a bite in the air that was keener than Bernie remembered for some time. It wouldn't be long now before winter was upon them.

She gathered some dry sticks and barrowed some cut logs from the woodpile in the shed at the back of the house. Then she lit a fire in the library and stood for a long while gazing into the crackling flames. Hot sparks and streams of smoke shot up into the wide, old chimney, just like my hopes for a happy future, she thought morosely.

At least cousin George had got in a big enough stock of wood to last for some time, so she didn't have to worry about heating bills. Besides, she rather liked the open fires. Together with the rest of the house, they made her feel as if she had stepped back into the past, into a calm, slow-moving, cosy world. It was good not to have all those modern-day reminders of her own past that had not been particularly happy.

Poor old George. She couldn't help often wondering if he had been a happy man during his comparatively short life. Always the shy, retiring bachelor, he had shied away from women. He had cared for his ageing parents until they died, and sadly he had followed them to the grave a few short years later.

As the room warmed, Bernie stopped shivering. She went to look out the window. The wind was whipping the last of the autumn leaves from the trees. Even the oaks were looking bare. A small, whimpering sound from across the room made her look up. Candy was sitting erect and expectant, one paw raised, ears lying back against her shaggy head.

'You want to go out, sweetie?'

Bernie went out into the hall, the dog

jumping excitedly around her ankles.

'OK, let's go. It's time we both had some proper exercise.'

Bernie carried the lead, but allowed Candy to roam freely. She was a good dog and usually came back when bidden. Besides, there was nothing to worry about, no traffic, no other dogs, no cattle, and any sheep there were usually kept to pastures 'way over the other side of the moors.

What Bernie liked about living here was that they could walk for miles and not see a soul. She braced herself against the force of the gale. It was so difficult walking she almost changed her mind and turned back, but the sharp, clean air would do her good, help cleanse her mind, and the walk might lift her spirits.

'Come on, Candy!'

The little dog was rummaging about in the small garden of the cottage. She zigzagged back and forth, nose to the ground like a remote-control vacuum cleaner! Her tiny stump of a tail was stiffly pointing to the sky and working overtime.

'What on earth's got into you, girl?'

Bernie finally managed to persuade the dog to come to her and slipped the lead on before she wandered off. Candy didn't appreciate the gesture and gave a deep-throated growl.

'That's enough of that, young lady. I'll let you off the lead when we get on to the moors and not before.'

Once on the moors, she kept her word, but Candy chose to stay close to her. She didn't like the wind and, out here in the open, where there was no sheltering hedge or coppice, it blew more fiercely than ever. Bernie pulled the hood of her anorak up around her ears and bent forward as she walked. She had to place her feet carefully on the rough ground with its mounds and hollows, its hidden rabbit warrens and its tufts of coarse grass that pulled at her ankles and attached itself to her trousers, threatening to trip her at every step.

'Isn't this great, Candy?' she laughed half-heartedly.

The dog turned its face up to her with an almost human expression that told her she wasn't exactly in agreement.

'It'll be easier when we go back. Then, we'll be walking with the wind behind us. Come on. Let's just go as far as that pile of rocks and then we'll turn around.'

But the pile of rocks was farther away than she thought. Candy's little legs were tiring. She would have to be carried back, no doubt. Fortunately, she hardly weighed more than a couple of bags of sugar, so that was no hardship.

They hadn't gone more than another few yards when Bernie's foot caught in a rut and her ankle twisted painfully. She dropped to her knees with a small cry and sat there trying to get her breath. The wind, ever more fierce, was making it almost impossible for her to breathe as it buffeted her face and her open, gasping mouth.

Candy had turned away from the wind and was jumping about and yelping and looking altogether like an unravelling ball of wool. Then there were two balls of wool and two strong hands were pulling her to her feet.

'Are you hurt?' a voice shouted in her ear.

She put her weight on the injured ankle and winced. Then she pushed back her hood which was preventing her from seeing her rescuer. Her heart did a swallow dive as she recognised her lurker. She flushed a deep crimson.

'What on earth are you doing out here on the moors?' she snapped ungraciously, pushing him away with both hands and nearly toppling as her feet found more ruts to sink into.

'The same as you, I suppose, walking my dog. Do you have an objection to that? Am I trespassing or something?'

Bernie scowled at him and automatically put a hand to her head, running shaking fingers through her tangled hair.

'No, of course not. It's just that you seem to keep turning up like the proverbial bad penny. I find it quite irritating.'

'I'm sorry you feel like that, because I feel quite the reverse.'

'What?'

'I find it immensely pleasing to keep bumping into you. You've made my visit to the north of England quite worthwhile.'

His mouth twitched and his eyes wrinkled with mocking laughter. Bernie sighed heavily.

'I can't imagine what you're getting at, and quite frankly, I couldn't care less. Now, would you please just go on walking your dog and get him away from Candy!'

'Mop! Come here!'

He scooped up his dog.

'Thank you,' she muttered through teeth clenched with anger. 'Now, would you please leave us?'

'Sorry? I can't hear you. The wind . . . '

He bent towards her and cupped a hand to his ear. She gave him a scathing look and tried walking away, but teetered painfully to one side and would have fallen again if he had not caught her.

'You can't walk on that foot. Hang on.'

He let go of his dog, which was perfectly happy to regain its freedom, and join his new-found love! Bernie glowered down at the two dogs, then gasped as she was unexpectedly lifted off the ground. The stranger had hoisted her in his arms as if she weighed no more than a sack of feathers.

'Put me down at once!' she shouted in his face and hoped that her anorak was thick enough to disguise the pounding of her heart against him. 'It's nothing! I'm perfectly capable of looking after myself, thank you very much.'

'Nonsense. You've sprained your ankle and if you walk on it you could damage it further. It's just lucky I was in the vicinity.'

Bernie wasn't sure whether his presence at that precise moment was due to luck or good management, but she clamped her mouth shut and said nothing. It was a strange sensation, being carried. She couldn't remember anybody ever carrying her, not even her father. It would have been almost a pleasure had it not been for the fact that her ankle throbbed with pain and the man doing the carrying was someone she was determined not to trust.

It didn't seem to take long to get back home. His long legs strode out purposefully, his feet planting themselves surely on the uneven ground. He was only slightly out of breath when they reached her drive.

'Please, put me down now,' she tried to insist, wriggling slightly in his arms, which made him tighten his hold. 'Look, I can manage the rest of the way.'

'For goodness' sake, woman, do stop fussing! And if you don't stop squirming like a slippery eel, I'll drop you.'

'But I want you to drop me. I mean . . . '

But her objections were all in vain. In seconds they were standing before her front door and he was lowering her gently, but still supporting her with a strong arm around her, pulling her into his side.

'Have you got the key?' he asked.

'I can manage, really. I don't want to keep you from . . . from whatever it is I'm keeping you from.'

Bernie dug into her pocket and produced the door key. She fumbled clumsily to get it into the lock. He took the key out of her trembling fingers and opened the door without any bother at all. Then he was helping her over the step and into the hall. She wanted to stop him, not allow him into her home, tell him she didn't want him anywhere near her and was that clear.

'Thank you. That's very kind. Would

you like a cup of coffee, or something?'

Bernie was appalled. She couldn't believe she had invited him to stay for a coffee! But to be honest, she would never have made it back home without a great deal of pain had he not helped her. So, she supposed, she had to show some gratitude.

'Yes, I'd like that fine, but you sit down and put that foot up and I'll make the coffee. Just tell me where to find the kitchen.'

'Oh, you'll never find things.'

'I assure you, I'm very good in other people's kitchens.'

He was already finding his way around and seemed to know exactly which door led to the library and where the fire was. He helped her to a chaise-longue, even lifted her foot with infinite gentleness and peeled off her anorak.

'Do you have ice in the fridge to put on your ankle?'

Bernie sighed. It seemed ridiculous to go on ranting and raving at him. He

31

wasn't going to take any notice. Besides, he seemed really rather nice and he had been an enormous help and . . . and he could turn nasty any minute and attack you!

She shuddered and hugged herself, trying valiantly to meet his hypnotic blue eyes without showing the whole gamut of emotions that were coursing through her body.

'I haven't any ice, but there may be a pack of frozen peas in the freezer that would do the job. The coffee and sugar are in pots on the work surface, next to the coffee machine, and there's milk in the fridge.'

'OK, now you just try to relax and leave everything to me, eh?'

'The dogs! Where are the dogs? I didn't see them come in with us!'

Bernie was suddenly frantic at the thought of losing Candy. That tangled mutt of his was probably at this minute leading the poor little thing astray. They were no doubt halfway across the moors by now and she might never see her beloved pet again.

'I'll check. Don't worry. Mop's a good little chap, really.'

He smiled down at her reassuringly, then left the room, following her directions to the kitchen.

Minutes passed and Bernie kept eyeing the telephone, wondering what to do for the best. That same sergeant was probably on duty again and he already thought she was a bit of a hysteric. What would she say to him anyway?

You know that lurker I told you about? Well, he's here with me right now, in the kitchen making coffee. And his dog's eloped with mine and I'm really rather worried about the whole situation.

Five minutes later, she heard his footsteps and the rattle of cups on a tray as he came back across the hall.

'Panic over! Our two furry friends are sharing a bowl of doggy nuggets in the kitchen. I didn't think you'd mind.'

'No, of course I don't, but . . . '

'Now,' he said as he put a mug of steaming coffee in her hand, 'what's the number of your doctor? I really think he should come and take a look at that ankle.'

He was already standing at the desk with the telephone receiver at his ear. Bernie stared at him and was tempted to tell him to go and leave her in peace, but if the man was prepared to phone her doctor, it seemed petty not to let him. She gave him the number and he made the call.

'Yes, Doctor, that's right. Probably nothing too serious. A sprain, I think. What's that? Ah, yes! Miss Brooks, Miss Belinda Brooks.'

'No!' Bernie exclaimed, shaking her head, but he had already hung up.

She was about to ask him how he knew her name, and also to explain to him that she was not, in fact, Belinda, but Bernie, or Bernadette, as she had been christened. Too many people were making this same mistake these days and it was beginning to annoy her intensely. She opened her mouth, then closed it again quickly as he looked her way. There was something odd happening here — strangers following her about, watching her every move, and this particular stranger seemed to know her name without asking, or thought he knew it, but was mistaken. Why? What was it all about?

'Good coffee!'

He was sitting on the end of the chaise-longue, having carefully placed a bag of frozen peas over her ankle, which had made her jump and shiver afresh.

'I'll have to try that brand. Now, if you'll excuse me, I'll be getting along. I have an appointment in town. I'll leave the door on the latch so the doctor can let himself in. He said he'd get here as soon as he could.'

And then he was gone, leaving Bernie wondering just what she was getting herself into. For one thing, there had been no sign of his car. Where had he parked it? And she didn't even know his name, though he purported to know hers, except he took her to be her sister.

Candy came into the room looking miserable. She jumped up on to Bernie's lap, curled up and went to sleep with Bernie's hand lightly caressing her.

'You fickle hound!' Bernie whispered. 'Fancy you disgracing yourself with that bundle of rags. You should know better. I'll have to have a girl-to-girl talk to you about not trusting strangers, especially attractive strangers.'

Four hours later the doctor had still not arrived. Bernie toyed with the idea of calling and cancelling the visit. Her ankle wasn't nearly as bad as she had thought at first. The frozen peas had got rid of the swelling and the pain was quite bearable, even when she put her weight on it. However, there could still be some damage, so perhaps it was better to do nothing and just wait.

Bernie, however, was not good at waiting. In order to allow her to move about more freely, she strapped up her ankle as best she could with some stretch bandage she found in cousin George's bathroom cabinet.

Thank goodness I'm not badly injured, she thought, glancing impatiently at the clock. I could be dead by now.

Candy suddenly shot out of the room and started making a fuss in the hall, yelping and growling. Normally, she was such a quiet dog.

'What is it, Candy? What's wrong, girl?'

The dog continued to fuss, so Bernie hobbled to the hall to see what the problem was, to find the front door wide open. She frowned at the gathering darkness outside. The wind was beginning to howl, bending the poplars on the drive almost double. Rain blew in, soaking the old parquet flooring. Water lay in shiny puddles. Bernie gasped, then remembered that the stranger had said he would leave the door open for the doctor.

A small, suspicious niggle started to grow in the pit of Bernie's stomach.

Had she been too trusting? After all, she hadn't heard the other end of the conversation when he had made his call to the doctor. A cold, prickling sensation spread over her body, making the hairs on her arms and the back of her neck rise. She quickly closed and locked the door. Candy had danced around her nervously, then shot off to the back of the house where there were old-fashioned pantries and the door leading to the cellar. That was where Bernie found her, sniffing at the bottom of the cellar door, quivering and yelping and looking altogether unnerved.

She wasn't the only one, Bernie thought. It was a huge cellar and Bernie would only ever go down to change electricity fuses. She couldn't understand what had possessed cousin George or the electricity board to install the fuse box in such an inconvenient place. Thank goodness she had not, as yet, been obliged to change a fuse.

Bernie stared at the cellar door and frowned. It was closed, but the bolt wasn't in place. She never left it like that. Normally, she kept it locked. Candy was behaving as if there was something or someone down there! Feeling deathly cold and frightened enough to scream, though no-one but the intruder, if there was one, would hear her, Bernie shot the bolt into place. She then marched back, limping slightly, to the library and picked up the phone, punching in the doctor's number.

'Dr Freeman's surgery. May I help you?'

'Sorry to bother you,' Bernie said, aware that her voice was shaking and that her knuckles were turning white as she gripped the receiver. 'I was expecting the doctor to call, but it's been four hours and . . . '

'What name is it, please?'

'Brooks. Bernadette Brooks. The Old Manor.'

'Well, I'm sorry, Miss Brooks, but there's nothing down here for you and the doctor's gone home. Is it urgent?'

'There must be a note there some-where. I . . . I mean . . . a friend . . . well, no a passer-by phoned in for me. I was out walking on the moors and twisted my ankle.'

'Well, I wasn't on duty four hours ago, Miss Brooks, but I assure you that the other receptionist hasn't recorded the call. I'm just about to go off duty myself, but if you're in pain I'll call the emergency service for you, or can it wait until tomorrow?'

'No, no, that's all right. Tomorrow will be fine, I'm sure.'

Bernie put down the phone and shivered afresh. He hadn't made the call. It was all a pretence. He had left the door open, not for the doctor, but for himself. No doubt it was that damned blue-eyed stranger she had trapped in the cellar. Oh, this was awful. Things were just going from bad to worse.

If she phoned the police and the cellar turned out to be empty, she would look such a fool. She just had to

40

be sure. If he was locked in there, at least he was out of harm's way. And, if it was, indeed, the man she thought it would be, his car had to be somewhere close at hand. Donning her anorak again and taking a torch, Bernie hobbled out into the storm and had to brace herself so as not to lose her precarious balance. Her ankle hurt, but she was determined to put it out of her mind. She stepped out into the road and looked up and down. No car.

Then she saw a light, a dull yellow glow, shining through the overgrown hedge that grew around the old cottage. Slowly, she crept forward, jumping as the gate creaked loudly when she leaned against it to catch her breath. The light was coming from a window at the front. Someone had rubbed a clean patch in the dirty pane. She went up to the window, tall weeds catching at her legs, rain soaking into the material of her jeans, running in rivers down her neck where she hadn't bothered to fasten her anorak.

Standing on tiptoe, she peered cautiously into the dimly-lit room and saw that the light was coming from a flickering oil lamp. There hadn't been any electricity in the cottage for years. There was a half-eaten sandwich on a plate next to an open notebook and some car keys. Otherwise, the room was empty. Bernie made her way around the cottage and there, in the tiny back garden was a silver grey saloon — the car that had followed her! His car. There was no doubt now in her mind. She had to call the police.

3

Bernie could not stop shaking. She hung on to Candy and the dog, sensing her mistress's anxiety, remained still and quiet, except, that is, for a low, gurgling growl when two black-suited police officers arrived to investigate Bernie's complaint of an intruder in the house.

'Now, miss, let's just keep calm, shall we?'

The older of the two officers placed his bulk before the warming flames of the open fire and gave her a benign smile.

'I am calm!' she said a little curtly, hugging the dog even more tightly to her. 'No, that's not true. In actual fact I'm terrified. Scared out of my wits, if you must know. I've been reporting someone following me and another man lurking around the place for about a month now and nothing has been done about it.'

'Well, we're here now, miss. There's somebody in the house now, you think, is there?'

'I know there is.'

She staggered unsteadily to a chair and sat down heavily with a painful wince as her injured ankle jarred.

'Had an accident, have you, miss?'

The younger officer, having finished his eye-ball check of the room, was now eyeing her with some speculation. He was probably resenting being called away from his cosy station in order to sort out the over-active imagination of one of the town's female residents.

'I was walking my dog on the moors,' she explained, gritting her back teeth to stop them chattering. 'He was out there today. He keeps on turning up, bumping into me as if by accident. And I think he's been keeping an eye on the house from the old cottage opposite. Nobody lives there. There isn't even electricity or running water. But he's been in there. There's a light burning and . . . and his car is parked in the back garden, all tucked out of sight as if he didn't want anybody to know he was there.'

'I see.'

The older constable exchanged curious glances with his colleague, rocked on his heels and sucked at his teeth in contemplation.

'Well, we'll take a look at the house now, if that's all right with you, miss?'

All right? She thought they'd never ask!

'Of course,' she said. 'But you need go no farther than the cellar. He's down there. I . . . I locked the door. There's no way he can get out.'

Again there was an exchange of curious glances. She told them where to find the door to the cellar and held her breath while they left her alone to investigate. It was spooky. Maybe he hadn't been alone. Maybe he had an accomplice lurking somewhere else in the house, someone waiting to do her harm after they had taken away the man with the blue eyes.

Ridiculous! Maybe, but even if the man in the cellar was alone, he could be dangerous. Despite his good looks and his charm, he looked as if he could be quite lethal if he chose to be. There was definitely a hardness about him somewhere. What if he had a knife or a gun? Ordinary country coppers didn't carry firearms.

He could kill the two policemen, then I'd be completely at his mercy.

Bernie stiffened as there was a slight scuffling in the hall, followed by voices and a hollow barking that made Candy quiver and emit a few yips of her own. Then there were angry voices raised. They echoed from the bowels of the house, but she couldn't make out the words.

She struggled feebly to her feet as heavy footsteps resounded across the hall. The two policemen entered the room first. The older of the two looked red-faced and sheepish. He was breathing heavily after negotiating the cellar stairs. The younger policeman seemed to be struggling with an emotion that strongly resembled laughter.

'Well? Where is he?' Bernie demanded.

'He's here!'

A deep voice that was already familiar to her ears reached her from the hall. Then the blue-eyed man appeared in the doorway behind the two officers of the law. He was covered with dirt and cobwebs and stiff with the cold. His handsome features now looked as if they had been carved from pure ice rather than stone.

'What's happening? What are you doing?' Bernie stuttered, looking from one to the other of them. 'Aren't you going to arrest him?'

'No, miss,' the older policeman said shaking his head. 'We can't do that. You see . . . well, there's been a bit of a misunderstanding.'

'A misunderstanding!'

Bernie was warming up now that her anger was beginning to take over.

'You call it a misunderstanding to find a strange man lurking in my house? A man I've already complained about? I don't believe this!'

'Then perhaps you'd believe this, Miss Brooks.'

The blue-eyed man shouldered his way past the uniformed officers and flashed an official badge in front of her bewildered gaze. She blinked at it, but couldn't focus on anything, except the letters C I D. She backed away and sank down again on the chair as her knees began to sag.

'I don't understand,' she muttered, her brow creasing.

He sighed, loud and long, then turned to the older policeman.

'Sergeant Darrow, would you please explain to this young woman exactly who I am? I have a feeling she wouldn't believe anything I tell her.'

'This is Detective Superintendent Glen Arden of the C I D, miss. He's on special assignment here to investigate a case of stalking.'

'So what is he doing shacked up in that derelict cottage, which also happens to be my property, watching my house and following me around? Surely, he should be out stalking the stalker, instead of acting like one himself!'

There was a short silence, then the blue-eyed man, who finally had a name, spoke again.

'I'm part of a surveillance team, Miss Brooks. My job is to protect you. To do that I have to stick pretty close. We haven't, as you seem to think, taken this thing lightly. Death threats should never be ignored.'

Bernie's mouth opened, then snapped shut again as his words sank in.

'Death threats! But I've not received any death threats. There must be some stupid mistake. OK, I reported a couple of incidents that scared me, but they never involved anything like a death threat.'

'We have it on file at the station, Miss Brooks. I can only presume you reported it.'

'I don't know what on earth you're talking about,' Bernie said with an exasperated sigh. 'Why should anyone want to threaten me? Besides, I don't know that many people around here. I only moved up from London a few weeks ago.'

Detective Superintendent Arden inclined his head and regarded her through half-closed eyes.

'This whole business is beginning to smell,' he said and he wasn't smiling. 'Do you expect me to believe that Belinda Brooks, the famous cookery expert who's never off the television, thinks she doesn't know enough people to be unpopular with one or two of them?'

Now she knew what was happening. She'd had this kind of thing before, but this was perhaps the worst yet in a long line of mistaken identity cases.

'No, I don't expect you to believe

that, because it's absolutely true. The thing is, Detective Superintendent Arden . . . '

She hesitated just long enough to enjoy the look of anticipation on his puzzled face.

'The thing is, I'm not Belinda Brooks. I'm her sister, Bernadette, some years younger, though it obviously doesn't show, and my cookery skills don't go much beyond opening a tin of baked beans. Would you like to see my birth certificate perhaps? Or perhaps we should just call my sister now and ask her to confirm a few facts.'

'Ah!' was all Arden seemed to be able to say.

Then, after a moment's reflection, he rubbed his hands together and blew on them. She noticed how his whole body seemed to be shuddering.

'In that case, Miss Brooks . . . Bernadette, not Belinda . . . it looks like we've all got egg on our chins and apologies are called for.'

He edged closer to the fire and she

suddenly felt very guilty and very sorry for having locked him in the cellar.

'Why didn't you tell me who you were and what you were doing?' she asked pointedly and got to her feet with difficulty.

The young constable rushed to help her with a steadying hand to her elbow.

'Where do you think you're going with that ankle?' Arden barked out. 'And why didn't the doctor dress it properly?'

'Because the doctor never got the call,' she informed him tartly. 'You know the one. The one you pretended to make while protecting me! I'm going to make a pot of tea to warm us all up.'

'No you're not!'

He reached out and grabbed her arm as she passed close by him. She toppled against his broad chest and he had to put his arms around her to steady her. It was such a secure feeling it might have been nice to stay there for a while, had it not been for the presence of the other two policemen.

'Meadows, go make yourself useful in the kitchen while the sergeant here reports in. As for me, since I'm officially off duty in five minutes, I'd appreciate a rather large whisky, if the lady of the house can run to that. No, Bernadette. You sit down. Tell me where it is and I'll help myself.'

'There's a decanter and some glasses in that cupboard between the book shelves,' Bernie said weakly as he pushed her firmly but gently down on to the chair. 'And please don't call me Bernadette.'

'I'm sorry if you think me too familiar, Miss Brooks.'

His face was serious, his eyes the darkened hue of a stormy ocean.

'It's not that. I just don't like my name. It makes me sound saintly and I'm anything but that, as my parents would tell you. Everybody calls me Bernie.'

'Bernie? OK, Bernie, if I may?'

She nodded slowly and saw his expression soften slightly, but his eyes were still wary.

'Do you think I could have a whisky, too, please? I feel a bit shaky.'

He poured out two generous whiskies and handed her one. They sipped simultaneously while eyeing one another above the rims of their glasses.

'I did speak to the doctor's receptionist, you know,' he said softly as the fire and the whisky thawed him out. 'She seemed rather flustered, but she promised to ask the doctor to call. However, please feel free to check it out. I certainly will.'

Bernie looked up at him with brimming eyes and an embarrassed flush burning up her cheeks as she explained, 'I thought you hadn't really spoken to anybody and then . . . and then you left the front door open so you could come back and . . . '

'What? Murder you? Attack you?'

Bernie blinked furiously as tears welled up in her eyes. She sniffed and

fumbled in her pocket for a handkerchief, but he was there with one of his,
all neatly washed and ironed.

'I'm sorry,' she said huskily and bit
her lips to stop from breaking down
into helpless sobs.

She hadn't done that since she was a
small child, not even when she split up
with Philip. Perhaps that in itself was an
omen. She hadn't cared enough even to
shed a tear. Maybe, if she was really
honest with herself, it had been
something of a relief to walk away from
an affair that had little to offer, past,
present or future.

'No need to apologise.'

Glen Arden bent towards her with a
sympathetic smile and pressed a large,
strong hand on her shoulder.

'At a guess, I'd say you've been
through quite a lot recently. Didn't
your sister tell you about the threats?'

She shook her head and blew her
nose, sure that it was glowing an
unattractive red beneath swollen eye-
lids. She must look perfectly ugly, she

thought, as she scrubbed her face with his no longer pristine handkerchief.

'We don't communicate much as sisters. Christmas, birthdays, and not even then sometimes. Belinda's far too busy. She has to rely on her secretary to tell her what day it is and what she's doing.'

'It's not easy being a celebrity,' Glen Arden acknowledged, then treated her to an attractive lop-sided grin that made her heart lurch, then change direction and go into a deep dive with his following words. 'My wife used to watch her show regularly. Unfortunately, the recipes never seemed to work out. We invariably ended up nipping out for Indian take-aways and fish and chips most of the time.'

His wife! He's married! And all that schmaltz and pseudo romantic talk! It was all for nothing . . . or maybe he thought he was on to a good thing on the side with me. Men!

'Thank you for the hanky,' she said abruptly, trying to hand the soggy square of white cotton back to him, but he indicated that she should keep it.

She stuffed it in her pocket and avoided his eyes.

'Well, if you don't need me any more . . . I mean, there's no point in following me about now, is there? I'm not the victim you thought I was.'

His eyes turned cool.

'If you'll just allow me to make a call, we'll leave you in peace.'

She nodded and watched as he took out a mobile phone and walked to the other end of the room with it pressed to his ear, talking into it in a low, official voice. He had removed his anorak and she noticed how well he filled out his sweater, how slim were his hips, how incredibly muscular were his long legs. Unlike Philip, who had gradually allowed his muscles to turn into flab over the years, this man looked as if he took the business of keeping fit very seriously.

If they had met in normal circumstances it would not have been difficult to allow him to flirt openly with her. There was something very sensual about Glen Arden, locked up in a tight spring, looking for release. She might easily have taken pleasure in providing him with that release, in normal circumstances, and, of course, if it weren't for the fact that she had sworn off men for the duration.

'Right! We'll be off, then.'

He was hovering, looking strangely reluctant to leave.

'Are you sure you're all right? Maybe you should call a friend to come and stay with you tonight.'

She shook her head quickly.

'As I told you, I'm quite new in the area and I doubt any of my London friends would want to make the journey just to baby-sit a neurotic pal.'

He smiled that devastating smile of his.

'I doubt if you'll be on your own for long, Bernie.'

He delved into his inner pocket and drew out a small business card.

'Here's my mobile number. Give me a call, if anything's bothering you. I'll come running.'

'Thank you.'

She put the card on the desk without taking much notice of it. It seemed wiser that way, more adult.

'I doubt if I'll have need of your services after tonight.'

'Well, anything's possible. Anyway, I'll be around for a while until we get your sister's case wound up.'

'I hope you get him, whoever he is. Belinda and I have never been particularly close, but she is my sister. I'd hate anything to happen to her.'

'We'll do our best.'

He nodded and started to leave, following the two uniformed men out of the room, but then he stopped, remembering something and swore softly under his breath.

'I seem to have lost one rather scruffy dog, who is the cause of this upset this evening. Mop has apparently fallen in love with your bitch. He ran off when I wasn't looking and I saw him disappearing up your drive with the wind in his sails. I tried not to disturb you when I followed him inside and down into the cellar. It would have broken my cover. Your dog wasn't there, but he always goes to ground when he feels his pleasures are being threatened.'

'I'm sorry I locked you in the cellar. I hope you don't catch a cold or something. But you really should have warned me . . . about everything.'

'I couldn't. You see, your sister is proving to be a rather difficult lady to protect. She refused absolutely to have anyone tail her. She said she couldn't have her private life spied on, no matter what.'

'That sounds very like Belinda. She's a free spirit. Doesn't like being tied down. Not even to save her life, apparently.'

'Well, this time that's exactly what it could do. Save her life. Ah, here's the little devil! Mop, you rascal. Boy, have you got something to answer for tonight.'

The scruffy male Yorkie cowered, quivering in the doorway, with Candy pushing up against him, nudging him affectionately and giving him sloppy kisses on his nose and his ear.

'Oh, Candy, stop that!' Bernie called out, but Candy went on regardless, deaf in her delirium.

Arden scooped up his dog, who growled with discontent, but knew better than to object too much.

'Mop, you lucky devil. I wouldn't mind a few of those candy kisses you've been getting.'

'Is that your wife's dog?' she asked in a voice too loud and far too over-confident.

He frowned, then shook his head.

'Paula doesn't like dogs. No, Mop and I kind of adopted one another one day as I passed by the dog pound. We haven't had time yet to get to know one another well but I'm working on that.'

Bernie made her face go blank. He

was pretending to talk about his relationship with the dog, when really his eyes and the way a smile played about the corners of his mouth, he was thinking of . . .

Don't be ridiculous! What would a man like Glen Arden want with you? He could have any woman he crooked his little finger at, married or not. If Belinda ever meets him she'll not hold back. He's just her type. Too good-looking to be true and unavailable in the long-term.

'Good-night, and thank you. I think I'll be able to sleep easy in my bed tonight after all.'

She let the sweep of her eyes include all three policeman.

She followed them out, said another gracious good-night and firmly locked the door behind them, pressing her back against it and letting out the longest sigh she had ever been able to produce.

Damn! He's married! Why do I always have to fall for impossible men?

4

But why on earth would they want to keep an eye on you!' Bernie heard her sister exclaim down the telephone.

It was typical of Belinda not to accept what she was told as gospel. It was also typical of her to get the wrong end of the stick. Her head was always so full of what was happening in her own busy life, she only listened with half an ear and even less interest to anyone else.

'There was no reason at all why they should be watching over me, Belinda. It was all a great big administrative mistake on the part of some new police recruit who somehow mixed our files, or at least, he transposed some of the details and your name and complaint ended up with my address. The C I D man in charge of the case phoned me up and explained it all. I'm afraid heads have been rolling. Just imagine, something terrible could have happened to you and all the while the people who were supposed to be protecting you were trailing the wrong Miss B. Brooks.'

'I still don't understand. I mean, why do they have your address on their files anyway? Have you committed some crime that we're all going to be ashamed of?'

'Don't be silly! Of course I haven't. It's just . . . well, about a month ago I put in a complaint about somebody following me. Of course, they took it all with a pinch of salt. I think they're all becoming a bit too cynical over women of a certain age.'

'Come off it. You're hardly out of your nappies.'

Bernie chuckled into the phone at her sister's words.

'I appreciate the thought, I think. And, Belinda, dear sister, I slipped out of my nappies long ago. For your information, the big three-o went by recently, though it was largely unnoticed by all and sundry.'

'You've had your thirtieth? I don't believe it! When?'

'A few days ago. In fact, I celebrated it by getting scared out of my wits because the whole of the police force mistook me for you.'

'Bit of an exaggeration, that, surely?'

'Yes, but that's how it felt on the night. Not only that, to make things even more embarrassing, I locked a detective superintendent in the cellar.'

'You didn't! Why, Bernie, I didn't know you were so anxious to find another man. What was he like?'

'To reply to your first remark, I'm not at all anxious. I've had enough of men for a very long time, if not for ever. In reply to your question about Detective Superintendent Glen Arden . . . '

She groaned.

'Well?'

'Gorgeous and married!'

'Why haven't I met him? He's on my

case, isn't he?' Belinda replied.

Bernie could detect a note of petulant jealousy in her sister's voice. Belinda, so sweetly seductive on the screen was, in real life, a voracious man-eater. At thirty-five she had been married three times and was constantly on the look-out. Happily, there were no children to suffer the consequences.

'It seems he came down with flu after the cellar episode, so they had to replace him. I'm not sure what he's doing right now.'

There was a rather unladylike grunt at the other end of the line before Belinda went on.

'Well, they replaced him with a fat boar of a man with a lurid sneer,' she told Bernie. 'He's perfectly grotesque and, I'm sure, completely incompetent. I could be murdered in my bed while he sits and reads girlie magazines in between asking me for recipes for his wife.'

'Belinda, why didn't you tell me that you were being threatened?' Bernie asked. 'It would have spared me a lot of bother.'

There was a short silence. She could hear her sister breathing heavily and heard a clicking sound that was probably Belinda's long fingernails tapping irritably on something hard.

'I don't tell my baby sister every-thing, you know,' Belinda said finally and Bernie could detect a note of fear, well hidden under a flippant attitude, but unmistakably there. 'I didn't tell anybody at first. You see, he left e-mails from a public computer. They were horrible. At first I thought it was just one of those crazy fellows who gets kicks out of shocking people. But then he started saying things that were more personal, things nobody should know. I finally had to tell the police. I was scared, you know.'

'But you still wouldn't let them put a tail on you,' Bernie broke into her sister's sudden flow of nervous words. 'Surely that's asking for trouble.'

'There's trouble and trouble, my

dear! If I tell you that I'm up to my neck in something that could ruin my career as well as my marriage, I'm sure you'd understand, Bernie.'

Bernie found herself nodding, even though her sister couldn't see her.

'Yes. I know you pretty well, Belinda. Don't you think it's time you settled down and gave your marriage a chance?'

'Oh, how boring! Look, I must dash. I have an appointment with my producer in half an hour.'

Bernie suddenly felt a strong urge to see her sister face to face. She couldn't explain it, but put it down to an acute attack of nostalgia.

'Wait, when can you come over for a meal, you and Edward? We haven't been together since the wedding.'

Bernie had been her sister's bridesmaid at each of her weddings. She was getting tired of pretending to find the old line amusing about always being a bridesmaid and never a bride. The sickening thing was, it looked like being true. It shouldn't bother her, she knew. Lots of women didn't marry from choice these days. She kept trying to convince the world, and herself, that she had joined their ranks. The trouble was, she was the one having difficulty believing it.

She heard Belinda's sigh and gritted her teeth against disappointment.

'Oh, Bernie, it's a lovely idea, but I have such a tight schedule and Edward's not too keen on social gatherings.'

'It wouldn't be a social gathering, just you and Edward and me.'

'Oh, haven't you found anybody to replace the handsome Philip? It always puzzled me how you managed to pick him up in the first place. I mean, you'd be far better off casting your net among the little fish rather than sharks and whales. Catch yourself a nice, ordinary little one. It's far more your style.'

Bernie closed her eyes, bit down on her lip and squeezed the telephone until her fingers hurt. That was Belinda all over. Just when you were feeling sisterly affection towards her she unsheathed her claws and scratched you where it hurt most.

'I wondered about Sunday lunch,' Bernie persisted coolly, keeping a hold on her rattled emotions. 'Surely even you don't work on Sundays.'

'Oh, but we have this cocktail thing at eleven. Odds are we won't be free until three or four.'

'Supper, then?'

Another long pause followed.

'Oh, very well. I'll try and drag Edward along.'

They agreed on eight o'clock and left it at that. As Bernie walked away from the phone, the doorbell sent a strident note echoing through the silent house. Whoever was pushing that button was doing so with some force, making sure they were heard. She pulled the door open, expecting to see a parcel delivery or some lost traveller wanting directions. What she wasn't ready for was a large bouquet of red roses, and behind them, Detective Superintendent Glen Arden!

'Hi,' he said casually but with a slightly embarrassed smile. 'I hope you like roses.'

He offered her the bouquet and she took them automatically, trying to look calm and collected, even though her heart was suddenly racing.

'I love them,' she said, keeping her expression cool, 'but why?'

'Just my way of saying sorry for all the upset I caused you recently.'

His smile widened as he looked at her, wrinkling the corners of his eyes. Bernie buried her face in the flowers and inhaled their heady perfume.

How was it possible, she wondered, to feel giddy with excitement and sick with apprehension both at the same time. It was going to come out all mixed up and look like irritability, and he would be immediately put off. Men didn't like irritable women.

'I can't pretend,' she said a mite too stiffly, 'that I wasn't frightened out of my wits. However, that wasn't totally your fault since I know now you weren't fed the correct details.'

'True. It says a lot for this computer age we're in, doesn't it?'

He was now pushing his visiting card at her, yet again.

'I know I've already given you one of these, but you probably filed it in the nearest wastebin. This time, I'd like you to hold on to it and . . . '

'And?'

She was aware that she was blinking at him rosily above the bouquet and he seemed to be finding something fascinating in her eyes.

'And I wondered if you'd be free to have dinner with me on Sunday evening.'

'Oh!'

Bernie gulped back her surprise, then a warning bell went off in her head. He's married, you idiot! Don't touch him with a barge pole!

'Well, it's very nice of you and your wife to invite me, but I'm afraid I'm going to be busy Sunday.'

'My wife?'

His brows dipped and his eyes darkened. Then he was shaking his head and his smile wasn't quite so wide.

'I'm not married.'

He couldn't help but notice her surprise, or maybe it was her relief that was shining through her perplexed expression.

'But I thought . . . ' she stuttered, crushing the roses to her chest, wincing as thorns bit into the flesh of at least four of her fingers. 'You said . . . '

'Oh, I see! When you suggested that Mop was perhaps my wife's dog and I told you . . . '

He laughed and scratched the back of his neck.

'My wife and I divorced about three years ago. Now, will you take my word for it and let me take you out to dinner?'

Bernie shook her head vehemently and tried to play for time while she figured out what she ought to do for the best. She had sworn off men not so very long ago, had almost convinced herself she hated every last one of them when it came to emotional involvement. And yet, here she was being invited out to dinner by this gorgeous hunk whom she had tried so hard to dislike and had failed miserably, so far.

'I'm sure you're telling the truth about your divorce, Mr Arden.'

'Glen, please.'

'Yes . . . er . . . Glen . . . but the truth is I am busy on Sunday evening, honestly. I've . . . '

She hesitated as an idea came to her that could be the ideal solution, or it could turn out a complete disaster, but she would have to take a chance on that.

'Actually, my sister and her husband are coming to dinner. We haven't seen each other in ages, so it's going to be a bit of a reunion. Why don't you join us? Or will it be frowned on? I mean,

74

mixing socially with the person in the case you're working on officially.'

Glen smiled broadly at that.

'Actually, I'm off the case as of now. I was only seconded on a temporary basis because there was a manpower shortage. The fact is, I'll be taking early retirement in December, so rather than take on cases that could be long-running, I opted to help out where and when necessary in between taking holidays owing to me.'

Bernie suddenly realised that she had kept him standing at the door and now moved back and invited him in, but he declined politely.

'Thanks, but, no. I have to attend a debriefing in town and I'm running a bit late.'

'Oh, well, see you on Sunday, then,' Bernie said, feeling decidedly shaky from the close look he gave her with those incredible blue eyes. 'Eight o'clock, OK?'

'Fine.'

He started back down the garden

path, then turned and grinned at her wickedly.

'You've got some courage, I must say, making a meal for one of Britain's number one cooks, even if she is your sister.'

Bernie gave a dry laugh, knowing that his words had struck home.

'Actually, the thought kind of paralyses my brain. I'd much rather take them out for a meal, but Belinda's too easily recognised so it takes away all the privacy. Besides, I can't really afford it. Don't worry. I'll open a few tins and hide the evidence. As long as she doesn't insist on my giving her the recipe I might even get away with it.'

'I'm a dab hand in the kitchen. Maybe I could come around early and help out.'

Bernie started to laugh, then realised that he was absolutely serious.

'Would you? Would you really?'

He nodded and gave her a deep, mock bow.

'At your service, madam. And I'll

bring the wine, unless you already have something special in.'

'Oh, no! That would be lovely. Thank you so much!'

He laughed again, raised a hand in goodbye and walked off, his long, muscular legs swinging, a slight bounce in his step.

Oh, dear! Now what have you done, Bernie, she thought. Maybe he's not as nice and sincere as he appears, and Belinda will no doubt take one look at him and steal him from under your nose. It won't be the first time she's walked off with your prize, my girl. Oh, stop crossing bridges before they're built. Inviting him with other people was a brilliant idea, even if the other people involved are Belinda and Edward.

Bernie took another long, exotic sniff at the roses and headed off to hunt down a suitable vase.

★　★　★

Bernie swiped the back of a hand across her forehead. It came away damp. She really ought to have another shower, she thought. She glanced at the kitchen clock and groaned. It was already seven o'clock and she was far from ready.

The main course, which had not in the end come out of a tin, was cooking nicely and the dessert was taken care of. However, she hadn't even begun on the starter and the table was still as naked as the day it was born, apart from a scattering of newspapers with job vacancies ringed, her feeble attempts to write an impressive application and a handful of negative replies.

Quickly, she tore open a packet of pre-cooked pastry cases, arranged them on a baking tray and put them in the oven. They only needed a minute or so to revive them before putting in the filling.

She was standing midway between kitchen and hall, trying to remember what it was she should be doing next, when the doorbell made her jump. Her stomach turned over as her heart rate increased. There was only one person who jabbed a finger on the button with so much authority and that was Glen Arden. She blew air out from puffed-up cheeks and wished it were possible to go back in time and do things again, only better.

She hadn't forgotten he was coming early, supposedly to help. It was just that the time had flown by unnoticed. Although she had showered half an hour ago, she was still in her housecoat, sleeves pushed up and a plastic apron protecting her. Her hair, although washed, was hanging about her face in a thick, damp curtain, looking decidedly uninteresting, and she was wearing a pair of thick, lambswool slippers that were warm and comfortable, but not exactly the last word in elegant footwear.

The bell shrilled again, followed by a sharp rap of knuckles. He wasn't the most patient individual in the world, she thought with a slight rise of irritation as she hurried across the hall and pulled open the door. The sight of Glen standing there looking so immaculate and handsome in a grey suit and white roll neck sweater made her feel even more gauche. And when he grinned and stepped over the threshold, brandishing more roses, white this time, and a bottle of Dom Perignon champagne, she realised just how small she was, standing before him.

'Oh!' was all she could muster. 'Please come in.'

'I'd say I've arrived just in the nick of time. You look as if you're in need of physical and moral support.'

Bernie closed her eyes and nodded.

'Actually, I need every kind of support that's going. Have you ever done something rash, then wished you hadn't, but it's too late?'

Glen looked thoughtful, but was having difficulty keeping the humour from his eyes.

'Hmm. I'm not known for rash acts,

but I think I know what you mean.'

He put the flowers and the champagne in her hands, then did something rash and uncharacteristic, or so it seemed to Bernie at the time. He leaned forward and kissed her forehead, just a light, butterfly touch, but her knees turned to jelly.

'I would really have preferred to kiss your cute little nose, Bernie, but at the moment it's covered in flour.'

'Oh, dear!'

Bernie rubbed furiously at her nose and felt her cheeks flame as he watched her, laughing. He had a nice laugh, deep and melodic, the kind that could be infectious. Then his own nose wrinkled and he sniffed the air.

'Is something burning?' he asked.

Bernie could smell the offending odour, too. Her eyes grew wide and her hand flew to her open mouth.

'Oh, no! My vol-au-vents!'

She flew to the kitchen, leaving him to his own devices. He appeared at the kitchen door as she was throwing away a full tray of rather blackened pastry cases.

'I must have turned the oven up to full power by mistake. Thank goodness my duck à l'orange is OK.'

'They say charcoal's good for the digestion,' Glen remarked lightly.

Bernie drew in breath, wanting to tell him to just stay out of her way and let her ruin dinner all by herself. However, the air was so thick with the smell of burning she nearly choked on a coughing fit.

'Well, that's the starter gone for a burton,' she said after she had downed a large glass of water. 'I hate to think what my sister would say if I serve her minestrone soup from a packet.'

'All is not yet lost,' Glen said, one finger raised to the ceiling. 'Have you got any salad?'

There was no problem there. Bernie practically lived on the stuff, winter and summer alike.

'But a plain salad isn't much of a starter for a cordon bleu cook,' she sighed, but he gave her a wink and a lop-sided smile.

'Not to worry! I brought my magic wand with me. Why don't you go and get ready? Take all the time you want and relax. This evening is going to be a great success, you'll see.'

It was strange the way she believed every word he said, as if he were someone she could trust and rely on — strange and nice, but at the same time, a little frightening.

5

What an awful fright she looked, Bernie thought as she glared at herself in the bathroom mirror. What must he think of her? There was flour all over her face, which was bad enough, but now she was all smudged with the black charcoal from the burned vol-au-vents! And just what she was going to do with the salad was anybody's guess.

She had meant to get some smoked salmon, just in case, but then she had forgotten. Belinda, of course, always kept a well-stocked cupboard, but then, she was never in the position of cooking for one. When you lived alone things tended to get out of hand. Besides, Bernie had always hated shopping. Crowded supermarkets with overflowing trolleys and sticky-fingered, wailing infants were not her favourite place.

So, now, she decided, we forget the

first course. Go straight into the main dish and act as if it was quite intentional.

Well, she couldn't do anything about it now anyway, so she might as well do what Glen had instructed. She would take her time getting ready and relax before the arrival of sister with husband number three.

I don't know why I'm worrying about the food, she thought. They'll probably still be under the influence of the midday cocktail when they arrive. They won't even notice the lack of a starter.

'And pigs can fly!' she sang out as she lingered under the soothing hot water of the shower.

Thank goodness she was pretty confident about the main course. That, at least, would be her saving grace. Although she always played down her ability as a cook next to the high standard of Belinda's culinary expertise, Bernie normally did things pretty well. She didn't particularly like cooking meals for her sister, but wasn't usually phased by the thought. No, this time, it had to have something to do with that ridiculously handsome police-man waiting for her downstairs. He had the kind of looks and subtle charm that made him irresistible.

She bit down on her smile as she remembered a description one of her friends had given of Tom Jones after watching him on television — a sex-bomb looking for somewhere to ignite. And she had made them all laugh when she told them that the singer, regardless of his advancing years, could ignite her any time he liked.

That's what had given her that breath-stealing blow to the solar-plexus the first minute she set eyes on Glen Arden. It had come in the guise of a shock to the nervous system and had frightened her silly.

'Damn him,' Bernie whispered to her reflection in the dressing-table mirror as she inspected herself.

Her hair had gone fluffy and refused

to lie down, but insisted on curling around her face in the thick waves her mother had been so proud of when she was a tiny child. Her eyes looked too glassy, her cheeks too flushed and her lips too full. The lilac angora sweater she had bought in a moment of weakness tickled her skin and moulded itself a little too intimately to her shape, giving her a provocative look. She thought of changing it, but really she had wasted enough time. It was already eight o'clock and there were still things to organise.

She sighed. Well, it would have to do. Please, she prayed, spraying herself liberally with perfume, please don't let them be too late. At least she could leave Glen talking to Belinda and Edward, lay the table and put the finishing touches to the meal while they made each other's acquaintance.

It would give Belinda more than enough opportunity to make a quick assessment of her little sister's new friend and decide he was worth stealing. That was unfortunate, but it couldn't be helped.

'Ah, there you are!'

He was standing in the hall, the bottle of champagne in one hand, a glass in the other.

'Sorry I've been so long,' she apologised, 'but you did say to take my time, and I feel so much better for it.'

She didn't think he would appreciate being told that she had dawdled on purpose so as not to have to spend too much time alone with him.

'It was obviously worth it. You look like a million dollars.'

He popped the champagne cork with his thumb and poured some of the sparkling liquid into her glass. He handed it to her with a knowing smile.

'Here, drink this. It'll give you courage.'

'Oh, but shouldn't we wait until my sister arrives? I mean . . .'

She was stuttering like a fool.

'I mean there might not be enough to go around.'

'All taken care of.'

Glen turned and headed back to the kitchen.

'There's another bottle in the fridge, and four bottles of wine taking up room temperature. Now, come and see what I've done while you were making yourself beautiful and tell me if you approve.'

Bernie followed him meekly, wanting to resent him making her feel like a stranger in her own house, yet secretly feeling that this was exactly the kind of thing she had always looked for in a man, the ability to take control. Her father had certainly never been able to do so. He always ran off at the slightest problem and was never to be found helping out in the kitchen. The casual boyfriends she had as a teenager wouldn't have known a teaspoon from a garden fork, and Philip, well, he certainly wasn't endowed with domestic skills. Come to think of it, she hardly knew any more what she had seen in him.

'Good heavens! What have you . . . ? Where did you . . . ?'

Bernie blinked in amazement at the four plates set out on the kitchen table. Her head snapped up and her baffled eyes narrowed, asking a silent question.

'It's French pâté. I go over to France as often as I can and stock up on the good things in life. I happened to have a jar of the stuff in the cupboard and thought you wouldn't mind if I contributed it.'

'But the whole thing looks so marvellous!' Bernie marvelled, unaware that she had reached out and squeezed his arm in gratitude.

'It wasn't a huge jar, so I used the filling you had for the vol-au-vents as a sort of dressing.'

Bernie laughed and shook her head in disbelief. The plates looked artistic and colourful, with the chicken and mushroom filling in a small pile next to a slice of pâté on a bed of shredded lettuce and with a tomato flower as garnish.

'I can't believe this! I really am grateful.'

She glanced at her watch and cringed.

'Oh, no! Quarter past eight! They should be arriving any time now.'

'Drink your champagne and calm down.'

Glen touched the bottom of her glass with his fingers and raised it up to her mouth. He watched her with a secret smile creasing his face as she sipped carefully.

'Don't you like champagne?'

'Oh, yes! It's just, well, it tends to go to my head and I haven't eaten all day. I'd hate to greet my sister and her husband in a drunken state.'

Glen threw back his head and laughed heartily and she found herself giggling along with him, the small amount of champagne already taking effect.

'I hardly think one glass of champagne will render you helpless. And even if it does, I won't take unfair advantage of you, much as I'd like to.'

He grinned and gave her a mock salute.

'Cop's word of honour, ma'am!'

She caught her breath as she felt her body start to melt when their eyes met.

No, Bernie! Stop this! He's just a man, isn't he? And you've already come to the wise conclusion that they're all horribly alike, especially the handsome ones.

'Look, I . . . '

She gulped down some more champagne.

'Glen . . . '

'Yes?' he interrupted.

'I'm sorry I treated you so badly. I mean, well, I really did think you were stalking me for some reason. There's been such a lot of that lately. It unnerved me a bit, especially coming after that other creep who followed me around.'

'What other creep?'

Glen's forehead creased.

'You know, the one I complained

about a few weeks ago. I reported it at the station. Mind you, they didn't take a lot of notice. I think they had me down as some kind of frustrated old maid.'

'And are you?'

'Am I what?'

He opened his mouth to reply and she could feel an embarrassed blush rising from her neck to her face because the conversation was heading in quite the wrong direction. However, before he could say anything more, the telephone rang and she quickly excused herself, relieved at being able to get out from under his blue gaze.

How silly she had been to use one of her mother's favourite expressions. Of course, the term old maid no longer existed in this day and age where women were free and independent. Nobody seemed to mind being single these days.

'Hello?'

Bernie snatched up the phone and fairly barked into it. It was Belinda, of course, full of apologies, but they couldn't come after all.

'Oh, no! But, Belinda, the meal's all ready and I've invited ... well, somebody else ... and it's going to be difficult! Can't you make it at all? Not even for nine o'clock?'

'Sorry, darling! Another time, when life isn't quite so complicated, eh?'

And she hung up, just like that. No more explanation, just a click and the purring of the empty telephone line. Bernie put the phone down, swearing softly under her breath. It was typical of Belinda to leave her in the lurch like this. Now what was she going to do?

'Problem?'

Glen was sitting sprawled in an armchair in the sitting-room beside a roaring fire when she joined him. He looked incredibly at ease and was helping himself to the nuts and olives she had placed in a bowl. He had Candy on his lap and was tickling her ear, which the little dog was accepting with shameless pleasure.

Bernie grimaced.

'I'm afraid my sister and her husband can't make it after all. I'm really sorry about this. If only she had phoned me earlier. I could have cancelled.'

'Well, I for one am very glad that she didn't.'

He put the dog down and got to his feet.

'Now, we can relax, enjoy dinner, which I'm sure will be superb, judging by the smell of things, and get to know one another.'

'Oh!'

'Come on, Bernie. Sit down and have another glass of champagne. Panic over, unless, that is, you would rather I didn't stay. You seem to be a little uncomfortable in my presence. You're not still scared of me, are you? I used to scare little girls when I wore a uniform, but that was a long time ago. Now, the little girls have grown up and don't find me half so terrifying. Well, what will it be?'

Bernie was blinking furiously at him, but her fury was directed at herself more than at Glen Arden. She wished he would go and leave her alone. Yet, on the other hand, she knew she would be rather disappointed if he did.

'Of course, you must stay, if you don't mind just having my company,' she said breathlessly and saw a slight shift in his tight features that told her he was pleased at her decision. 'It would be a shame to waste all that food, after all, and your pâté. It really was kind of you to think of it. Belinda would have been very impressed.'

'Just helping out a friend,' he said with a lop-sided smile. 'We are friends now, aren't we, Bernie?'

She hesitated, her heart palpitating. There was no way she wanted him to take her answer the wrong way.

'Yes, of course. Well, I suppose I'd better go and lay the table.'

He cleared his throat and the lop-sided smile returned.

'I took the liberty of doing that for you. I hope you don't mind.'

'But how did you . . . I mean . . . '

'Everything was easy to find. You're very methodical in the kitchen, Bernie, very efficient. I like that.'

'What was your wife like in the kitchen?' Bernie asked, silently kicking herself because she had promised not to bring up any questions about his private life, especially questions about his ex-wife.

'She was nothing like you,' he said thoughtfully, his eyes darkening. 'Not in any way, shape or form.'

Bernie wasn't sure if that was good or bad. She was glad she didn't remind him of his wife, but then again she didn't know if that was a plus or a minus. She gave him a tight, little smile.

'Shall we eat?'

Bernie was surprised and delighted when they entered the dining-room. The table was attractively laid with the best linen, silver and china. He had even arranged the bouquet of white roses neatly in a vase and found some white candles, which he now proceeded to light with a silver cigarette lighter.

'I didn't know you smoked,' Bernie said, for want of something to break the embarrassing silence that had descended all around her.

'I don't any more, but I always carry this about with me. You can see how useful it can be.'

'It's a far cry from the Boy Scouts, but at a guess I'd say you came out with all flags flying, or all stars twinkling, or whatever it is they award Boy Scouts.'

He chuckled and finally succeeded lighting each candle.

'I wouldn't know. My mother gave me all the training she felt I would need. Much as she loved . . . still does love . . . my father, she has always felt that her life was sadly lacking in romance. She drummed it into my brothers and me from a very early age just exactly what women like in a man.'

'Not all of them, surely! We can't all like the same attributes in our ideal partners.'

Bernie brought in two plates of the pâté starter and they sat down, one on either side of the rather grand dining table. They were close enough to look at each other, but not touch, she thought practically.

'Ah, that's been my downfall, in a way,' he said and studied her carefully. 'The story of my life is that I attract the wrong type of woman. My wife, for instance, was disorganised, untidy, couldn't cook and yet resented me interfering in the kitchen, or anywhere else that she thought was her domain.'

'But you loved her?'

It was a rhetorical question and she saw his eyes narrow before he replied.

'I thought I did. It seems I was wrong.'

'Did she love you?'

Why did her stomach turn over in anticipation of his answers regarding his wife? It was ridiculous. It was also none of her business, but he looked at her a long time, a forkful of pâté half raised to his mouth.

'No,' he said and shook his head eventually. 'No, I don't think she did. In fact, I'm certain she didn't. She liked to show me off to her friends. The prize stallion.'

'Do you have any children?'

Again a shake of the head and a shadow flitted over her face that made Bernie wish she had never asked.

'There was a child. She lost it.'

'I'm sorry.'

'It was for the best in the long run. Paula didn't want children really. She just omitted to tell me how she felt before we got married.'

'Would it have made a difference? I mean, would you have still married her?'

Bernie couldn't stop the questions flowing. She needed desperately to know more about this fascinating man who just had to look at her to make her toes curl.

'I'm not sure now, but at least I would have gone into the marriage with my eyes open. How about you, Bernie? Have you ever been married?'

Bernie shook her head briefly.

'I had a long relationship with the wrong man and should have known better. He was married, I discovered, and never really intended to divorce his wife in my favour, no matter what he kept telling me. I believed him for a while, but it never happened. He always got cold feet and ran back to her. Then I saw them together one day with their children. They looked so normal, so happy. I couldn't believe that he would risk everything he had, not even for me. I didn't know he was married when we first started dating. By the time I found out, our feelings had grown too much to back out. At least, that's what I felt at the time. I know now I was wrong. I've felt guilty about it ever since and I wish there was some way I could make it up to his family, but I don't think they were even aware of my existence. Silly, isn't it?'

Glen put down his knife and fork, slowly wiped his mouth with his napkin and shook his head.

'No, Bernie. It isn't silly at all. Life

sometimes has a nasty habit of tying us up in tight, little knots. Maybe we see the problems coming, but we block them off because we're all blinded by the same dreams, the search for happiness, for love, something to make our lives more bearable. It's human nature to dream, just as it's human nature to make mistakes.'

Two hours later they were still talking, still exchanging notes on their personal lives. Bernie felt she had known him for ever and she saw a different side to him than the one he portrayed to the public, the one that made him a cold, hard-nosed police-man with a rakish smile.

He was actually kind and under-standing, philosophic and surprisingly good-humoured. He told her he came from a large, extended family and she was envious when he said how close they all still were. His nephews and nieces were numerous and he obviously adored them all.

'My family gives me a lot of stick. I'm

the only one not married, the only one without children.'

'But you were married, to Paula!'

'Somehow they don't count that. She never really fitted in. They thought her a bit of a cold fish and too much of a snob. You must meet them one day. I have a feeling they'd approve of you.'

Bernie stared unblinking at his remark, not daring to attach too much meaning to it. Things seemed to be rushing ahead too quickly. She pressed a hand to her midriff to settle a flurry of butterflies and swallowed with difficulty because her throat had suddenly dried up.

'Would you like some more dessert?' she croaked, reaching for her glass and pouring in a large amount of water.

She felt she had drunk far more wine that evening than was wise. Glen groaned and leaned back in his chair, patting his stomach.

'I couldn't eat another morsel. Bernie, I don't know why you were so worried. The meal was delicious. I've never tasted duck like that in my life, and the potato Dauphin was absolutely superb. The French would be proud of you. As for the meringue — wicked!'

'Perhaps you would like a glass of port with your cheese in the library?' she suggested, rising to her feet and having him meet her at the end of the table. 'I'll bring some coffee, too.'

'That sounds very grand.'

'Well, my cousin, who inherited this house from previous generations of the Brooks' family, didn't believe in changing anything. He wasn't rich, by any means, but there is a library and it is well stocked. It's also my favourite room and possibly the cosiest room in the house.'

'I see.'

'So, would you like to have coffee there?'

'There's just one thing I'd like to do right now,' Glen said, his voice becoming slightly gruff.

'Oh?'

Bernie's skin tingled as he moved

closer and put his hands on her shoulders, drawing her close, then running his hands down her arms.

'I'd like to kiss the hostess, if she doesn't mind.'

6

Bernie felt panic rising at a suffocating rate as she felt the touch of his lips on hers, so feather light, so fleeting, she could hardly believe it had happened. She looked up in time to see raw desire begin to kindle in Glen's blue eyes as his head descended a second time.

This time she gasped as her whole body was gripped in some kind of electrical, pulsating shock. It had never been like this with Philip, never this totally engulfing surge of passion that coursed through her body like fire.

'Please, stop!'

Glen was looking down at her, clear disappointment in his face.

'I thought . . . '

'That we were friends? Yes! All right, friends. But not . . . not this . . . '

Bernie waved a hand helplessly before her face and turned away from his questioning gaze.

'I think perhaps for both our sakes you'd better go.'

He hesitated, a long pause, when he seemed to be struggling for words. When he finally spoke, his voice was strained.

'Bernie, I really am sorry. Obviously, I misunderstood your signals. My fault entirely. Look, I just want to tell you . . . '

'Please, Glen! Please! Just leave!'

'But . . . '

'No!'

She hurried out of the room to the hall, pulled his coat from the cupboard there and thrust it at him, shaking her head, ashamed of the tears that streamed ridiculously down her cheeks, and angry at her own reactions. Angry, and, oh, so humiliated. She couldn't even bear to watch him go, because she might be tempted to change her mind and call him back. She had made that mistake once before. She wasn't prepared to fall into that same trap a second time. Anyway, he was probably spinning her a few untrue yarns about his marriage and his family, and everything!

There was something very true in the old adage — once bitten, twice shy, only in her case, it was thrice bitten, if she counted what her father had done to her mother. Glen wasn't exactly dim-witted. He had probably worked out very quickly that she was a stupid, gullible woman and ripe for taking advantage of, just like Philip had done, only with Philip, she had been stupid enough to get caught.

Glen Arden, why did you have to go and spoil such a marvellous evening? Why couldn't you have just left things on a friendly basis?

Bernie cleared the dining table and started washing up. She clattered the dishes unnecessarily. Her hands were clumsy because of her emotional state and when she broke a plate she swore loudly and kicked out at the pedal bin, not that it gave her much satisfaction.

The thing spilled over and she had to fight Candy over the contents that spread themselves over the kitchen floor.

It was well after midnight when she finally hauled herself up the stairs to bed. She felt exhausted, yet she knew she was unlikely to sleep that night. In fact, she suspected that a whole string of sleepless or disturbed nights was already lining up for some time to come. On the small landing at the top of the stairs, she paused to gaze out at the full moon. It was huge, almost like a harvest moon and tinged with orange. The light from it spilled over the land, drawing a silvery outline around the trees and the buildings, bathing the distant moors in an ethereal glow.

As she looked, she thought she saw something move out of the corner of her eye, something down in the garden. She peered out, her nose pressed up against the glass. Whatever it was had been no more than a fleeting shadow. A cat perhaps, or a stray dog, prowling around looking for supper leftovers, she decided. She looked down at her feet and smiled ruefully at Candy sitting there with mournful eyes. The Yorkie raised a paw and whimpered plaintively.

'Oh, goodness, you haven't been out tonight! Come on, girl.'

Bernie turned and headed back down the stairs, the dog keeping pace with her at every step. She pulled on a coat in passing through the hall, picked up a torch and stepped out into the semi-darkness. The dog scuttled off to investigate a few corners of the garden before settling down for the night. It was a ritual she enjoyed and she usually made the most of it.

'Candy! Where are you? Come back, you naughty girl!'

Bernie had seen the tiny silhouette dart across the drive and out on to the road beyond. Normally, the dog kept within the perimeter of the garden. However, that evening had not been normal for either of them. Bernie shivered as she picked her way down the lane, shining the torch from left to right. The dog was nowhere in sight.

'Oh, this is just too much!' she muttered under her breath.

She retraced her steps and gave a sigh of relief at the sight of Candy sitting halfway up the drive waiting for her as if butter wouldn't melt in her mouth.

'Pest! Get back in the house!'

Candy made a fuss once inside the hall and scuffed and snuffled at the library door, then went and did the same to the sitting-room door. Bernie couldn't help grinning to herself as she picked the dog up and took her through to the kitchen where she had her bed.

'Be a good girl and go to sleep,' she ordered, putting the dog into her basket.

She then left her, shutting the kitchen door behind her. Given a choice, she knew Candy would want to spend the night with her, curled up at the end of her bed. On occasions, when she had forgotten to close the door, she had found her there in the morning. But much as she loved the animal, she didn't want her in the bedroom.

It was ten to two when the noise startled Bernie. She hadn't exactly been asleep, but drifting in and out of a troubled slumber. So the noise when it came, made her sit up with a stifled cry and a pounding heart. What had it been? Something falling? A door slamming? What? She sat listening, her heart beating madly up into her throat. Nothing. She lay back down and was just beginning to drift off again when another sound reached her ears, a floorboard somewhere, creaking.

Suddenly, she jumped up as a burst of high-pitched, excited yelping came from Candy in the kitchen. She was basically a quiet dog, not given to outbursts in the middle of the night, which made it all the more worrying. She tried not to panic. There were always strange noises to be heard in the silence of the early hours. Old houses were like that.

There it was again, like a heavy foot being placed with care on worn, uneven timbers. Where was it coming from? Somewhere downstairs, she thought. All the floors in the house creaked when walked on, but the library was the worst. There was definitely someone in the house!

Fumbling around in the dark, now that the moon had hidden itself behind thick cloud, Bernie struggled into her dressing-gown. She crossed to the door, pressing her ear against it to see if she could hear any more noises. There was just the odd tiny woof from Candy, who was probably quivering with fright in her basket by now.

Knowing that she would have to investigate or she would never be able to settle in her bed, Bernie looked about her for a handy weapon if needed. The first thing that came to hand was an antique, long-handled warming-pan. She took it down from the wall and balanced it in her hands. Then she carefully opened her door,

113

wincing at the slight metallic rattle of the brass handle and the creak of the old hinges. Placing one bare foot slowly before the other, she made her way slowly downstairs.

Standing in the middle of the hall, she glanced around blindly, hoping that her eyes would soon adjust to the darkness. Then she saw it. The library door was ajar and she had definitely closed it. The hair on the back of her neck stood up and her flesh started to crawl as she inched forward. She halted just inside the doorway as another creak of the floorboards reached her. Biting hard on her bottom lip to stop her from screaming, she took a deep breath and eased her way stealthily into the room, her bare feet making no sound, but her heart pounding loud enough to raise the rafters.

Just then the moon decided to show its face again and it lit up the figure of a man standing with his back to her. She didn't stop to think. The bed-warmer rose and fell with a resounding thud, bouncing off the intruder's head. He fell to his knees with a short grunt, then ended up sprawled full length at her feet.

Bernie couldn't believe it. She'd actually knocked him out, whoever he was. She reached over him and snapped on the desk light, then stood back and gasped as she recognised the unconscious figure — Glen Arden!

What on earth was he doing back here in the middle of the night? Could it be that he had been stalking her after all, as she had at first suspected? Had he just been charming to weave his way into her heart so he could . . . so he could what? He couldn't plead a case of mistaken identity any more. He knew now which sister was which.

The thought that she might have killed him suddenly gripped her and she bent over him. He moved slightly and groaned when she prodded him. At least he was still alive. But what on earth was she going to do with him now? Oh, this was a fine mess and no mistake. She could just imagine the response of the desk sergeant at the police station. And he would go off into peals of laughter and treat her like some mental defective, which she was fast becoming.

A knocking noise made her jump and set Candy off yelping and howling. This time the noise had come from above her head, from one of the spare bedrooms, and this time, she knew, it couldn't possibly be Glen Arden. Perhaps there were two of them after all, Arden and his accomplice. Whatever the explanation, there was certainly somebody else in the house. It was unlikely she would be lucky with the warming-pan a second time.

Bernie started to step around the body on the floor, but at that moment Glen stirred and raised himself up on one elbow and squinted up at her, groaning.

'Bernie! Upstairs! I saw him climb in. Oh, God, what hit me?'

She went down on her knees. There

was something so innocent in the expression on Glen's face and in his words that her heart went out to him.

'Oh, Glen! I'm sorry! I heard something, somebody. When I saw you standing there in the dark, I thought . . . well, it doesn't matter what I thought. What's happening for goodness' sake?'

'I wish I knew,' he muttered through gritted teeth as he struggled to get to his feet.

Bernie got up with him, hanging on to support him, and also because her own legs were threatening to give way. Something made them both look towards the door in unison at some unidentified movement or sound. There was a blinding flash of bright white light that made them call out and blink furiously.

'What the . . . '

A shape appeared in the doorway, a stocky character with a sleazy grin and lank, oily hair hanging over his face. He pushed it back with a thick hand and gave a low, earthy chuckle.

'Nice pose, Mrs Terry. Just what your husband ordered! But I must say it's taken some getting.'

'Who on earth are you and what are you doing breaking into private property in the middle of the night?'

Glen stepped forward as he spoke, on unsteady legs, one hand exploring the lump Bernie had put on his head.

'Don't come any nearer than that, sir!'

The man took a step back and they could see what had caused the blinding flash now. He was carrying a camera, an old-fashioned reporter's one. He was dressed in a shabby raincoat with the belt tied tightly about his middle. Maybe he had seen better days, but it was doubtful.

'I know who he is!' Bernie exclaimed, tugging at Glen's arm, not wanting him either to get too close to the other man, or get too far away from her. 'He's the man I complained about, the one who kept following me about. The first one, that is. Nobody would believe me at the time, but that's him. I'm sure of it.'

She heard Glen's sigh, saw the slow, sickening smile of the man with the camera.

'Right, whatever your name is, stay right there. I'm arresting you.'

Glen flashed his identity.

'Hey, you're not going to cop me, mate! You're the one in trouble here. It wasn't my idea to break in and take photographs of the happy couple. It was the lady's husband. I'm a respectable private detective. Carter's the name, Barry Carter.'

Glen glanced over his shoulder at Bernie who was watching with wide-eyed amazement.

'Bernie?' he began, seeking some explanation.

'But I'm not married!' she almost shouted out with frustration.

'Who is it exactly you're supposed to be following and photographing?' Glen asked Carter grimly.

The other man sniffed and pulled at his ear.

'Her,' he said, indicating Bernie.

'For what reason? Divorce isn't so difficult to come by these days. Why would he want to take photographs?'

' 'Cos he's fed up with her nonsense. Wants to put a stop to it. I suppose you could call it a bit of emotional blackmail. She thinks more of her public image than she does of her husband, so he figured if he threatened her with exposure, she might think twice about taking on another extra-marital pastime. If you get my drift.'

Glen raised an admonishing finger, then clasped a hand to his head and sank to his knees. The photographer took that moment to make a run for it.

★ ★ ★

When he arrived in response to Bernie's call, the doctor looked rather irritated to be called out in the middle of the night. He made a quick

120

examination of the patient and diagnosed a slight concussion. Two days' rest was prescribed, and no driving.

Glen spent the rest of the night in the spare room. Bernie locked herself in her own room, with Candy for company and moral support.

The following morning, Belinda was on the phone bright and early. Had Bernie seen the morning's papers? What a hoot! Edward was furious, of course. It made him out to be such a fool, thinking that it was his wife who was liaising with the local police force! Then he took a better look and saw it was her look-alike sister after all. He'd gone positively grey about the gills thinking of all that money he'd wasted on a private detective.

'Many thanks, Bernie, for the cover story!' Belinda said in great delight.

'I'm sorry, Belinda.'

Bernie yawned and rubbed her eyes, tired and red-rimmed from lack of sleep.

'It's all been such a ridiculous

mix-up. And, by the way, I am definitely not liaising or whatever with Glen Arden or any other member of the police force!'

'Oh, don't worry about it, darling!'

Belinda seemed unusually cheerful considering the fact that her career could have been spoiled because of what the newspapers had published about her.

'As they say, any publicity is good publicity. I'm now notorious as well as famous. Poor Edward, though. He paid that reporter a small fortune, apparently, and the fool couldn't even get the right woman. All the time he was tailing you he thought it was me, silly fool. Edward said he never gave him the address because he didn't want him hanging around the house, just assumed the fellow would follow me from the studios. As you know, I never conduct my affairs from my home base. That would be just too crass, wouldn't it? Tell me, Bernie, darling, you're not really contemplating having an affair with that gorgeous hunk of a detective, are you? I mean, he's really not your type, is he?'

'We're just friends, as they say in your circles,' Bernie replied through gritted teeth.

Then she cringed as she thought of that photograph of her in her housecoat clinging on to Glen. Half the local populace would be looking at it now and making up their own stories.

'Sure you don't fancy him?'

She could almost hear the wheels turning in her sister's crafty brain.

'I couldn't be more sure, Belinda.'

'I'm so glad to hear that, because he's back on the case apparently.'

'What?'

'He's going to be my watch-dog. I'm still getting threats from a member of my adoring public. It's quite frightening, really. It'll be such a relief having Glen Arden as my shadow.'

'Well, it won't be for long,' Bernie countered. 'He's retiring soon. He's going to take up art and open a field study centre. It's something he's always wanted to do. He only joined the police force to please his father.'

'Really? How interesting. Maybe I'll persuade him to paint my portrait, and take a lovely, long time doing it.'

They said goodbye and Bernie sat for a long time, nursing the phone in her lap, staring into empty space and wondering just where she had gone wrong. She had taken a breakfast tray to Glen earlier. He claimed to have a slight headache, but otherwise was all right. However, his attitude seemed flat and dull. He had not mentioned last night and she wondered if he had acted a little too rashly because of the champagne and too much wine to follow, showing his feelings too rashly.

7

Glen chose to ignore the doctor's advice. It was obvious that he had no desire to spend any more time than absolutely necessary under the same roof as Bernie. He made the excuse that he was feeling fine and there was a lot of work waiting to be cleared up on his desk, and a certain private detective to be checked out.

'I'm going to take his licence and throw it to the lions!' he growled caustically, touching the tender spot on his head. 'That is, if he actually has a licence, which I doubt.'

They were standing in the library by the window as they talked. Outside, the sky was laden with dark storm clouds and somewhere close by there was a continuous rumble of thunder. Bernie watched, fascinated, as a sprig of variegated ivy waved about in a sudden gusting wind. It looked like it was waving at her, giving her some kind of signal. She didn't know what the signal meant, so she didn't know how to respond. She felt as if her brain was dead, her body paralysed, her heart in some kind of limbo.

'My sister says you'll still be working on her case. You know, tailing her and all that kind of thing.'

The words came out flatly and her mouth was dry.

'Oh? Perhaps. I don't know.'

They were talking together like two strangers on a train who would separate and not even say goodbye. In five minutes they would forget they had ever met.

The thunder was drawing closer and in the east the sky was lit from time to time with shards of lightning that illuminated the moorland. To the northwest there was a dark, ominous rain cloud.

'When I was a little girl,' she said, half to herself, 'I used to think that storms were when God was angry and rain was the tears of the angels. The wind was a brush that swept away the bad things and the sun was Heaven smiling on me. And I thought rainbows were dreams that were always going to come true.'

'And did they?'

He came closer and his voice was now softly caressing, though he refrained from touching her.

'Did your dreams come true, Bernie?'

She shook her head and gave the gathering storm a wry smile.

'They don't, you know. Dreams, I mean. They don't come true. They just keep you going, then make a fool of you at the end of the day.'

'Sometimes they come true, Bernie, if you let them.'

She glanced up at him and turned away quickly, not wanting to fall under his spell.

'I've tried,' she sighed. 'But it always leads to disillusionment.'

'Always is a long time, Bernie,' he

said, suddenly more serious than she had ever seen him. 'You're still a young woman. Don't give up on life before you've given it a second chance, or a third, if necessary.'

'I think you'd better go now, Glen,' she said, her eyes still fixed on the darkening horizon. 'It looks like being a big storm when it comes. I wouldn't like to think of you driving through it.'

She had given up reminding him that the doctor had advised he shouldn't drive for a while. He followed her gaze and out of the corner of her eye she saw him nod.

'I just have some things to collect from the old cottage, if I may?'

She looked at him and frowned, then remembered that he had used the cottage as an undercover lookout post. 'Yes, of course.'

'Well,' he began and held out his hand to clasp hers tightly when she took it. 'I'll say goodbye. Take care. You've got my number, in case.'

She nodded sharply and looked away,

her eyes filling with tears.

Stupid! Don't show that you care! It's the one thing he's looking for, she kept saying to herself.

'Goodbye, Bernie,' he said again and then she heard his footsteps and the door close.

She continued to stare at the stormy landscape beyond the window until her tears mingled with the rain that spattered on the panes. Had she been a fool to let him go? How would she ever know?

She turned from the window and called to Candy, but the dog didn't come running as she usually did when her mistress called. She had been behaving quite irrationally lately. At that moment the sky darkened as the storm broke directly overhead. Lightning and thunder fought it out, reverberating around the old house, making the rafters tremble, the windows and china rattle like fear-ridden, chattering teeth.

'Candy?'

Her heart sinking at the thought of

the little dog being out there in the storm, Bernie did a systematic search of the house, then donned a long waterproof and ventured outside. The whole landscape was being torn apart. She had never seen such a wild, vicious storm. She pulled up the hood of the waterproof, but the wind whipped it away again, so she ignored it and ploughed forward, looking this ways and that, calling her dog's name in vain.

Poor, dear little Candy. She was too small to be out on a day like this. One good gust of wind would sweep her away. Bernie stood in the road, shading her eyes against the onslaught of the torrential rain. There was certainly no sign of any living creature, nothing, except the glow of an oil lamp from the cottage where Glen was collecting his papers and whatever else he had stored there.

As she was debating which way to go in her search for her beloved companion, there was a blinding flash and an enormous, ear-splitting explosion as the lightning hit the old elm tree that sheltered the cottage.

'No!'

Bernie screamed out the words and ran forward, not thinking of anything but the safety of Glen who was inside. The tree shattered at the base, bursting into flames as it went down, falling, oh, so slowly and with a terrible groaning, right through the roof of the cottage.

Bernie fell to her knees in the mud, her hands covering her mouth to stop her from screaming hysterically. Glen was in there. There was a tree now flattening the whole cottage, razing it to the ground. Cement and stone dust rose in a dense, choking cloud. The bole of the elm tree was all aflame, flames leaping into the air. It was soon an inferno.

It's all my fault, she thought. I should never have sent him away. If I'd let him stay he would be alive now. He'd be standing here beside me, watching this spectacle.

Bernie flew like a leaf on the wind

back to the house and called the fire brigade, then she raced back to the scene of devastation. The cottage had, blessedly, not caught fire. Perhaps the rain had been too torrential and had not allowed the old stone to ignite. She ploughed forward, gasping, gulping in smoke-laden air, coughing and spluttering, dreading what might present itself before her frightened eyes.

'Glen!' she screamed, in the hope of hearing an answering call that would tell her at least that he was still alive. 'Glen!'

There was no-one there! Bernie sifted through the rubble, her hands, her fingers, bruised and grazed. She felt no pain. She pulled at beams, threw aside stones, kicked out at bits of wrecked furniture. He wasn't there!

She staggered back out on to the road and saw something moving through the mist. Somebody was walking up the road from the moors, somebody with head bent against the storm.

'Glen?' she screamed out frantically.

The person stopped and a hand was raised. She ran forward.

'Glen!'

His face was blanched white with the cold, but his eyes were alive and so was he. She threw herself bodily at him.

'Oh, Glen! I thought you were dead!'

'Whoa!' he shouted through the clatter of the thunder and the wind.

'Careful there!'

Then she saw two tiny, bedraggled faces peeping at her furtively from the safety of his anorak — Candy and Mop! She fell on them both with kisses.

'These two wretches decided to go walkabout and picked the worst day of the year. I had the devil of a job catching them,' he explained.

Then, before she knew what she was doing, she was clinging to Glen and kissing him as if kisses were going out of fashion.

'Well, that's great, but I'd like to know what I did to deserve a change of heart,' he said, holding her as tightly as he dared, with the two dogs clamped between them.

'Oh, Glen, the elm tree fell through the roof of the cottage and I was sure you must be dead!'

Her words spilled out and she was crying profusely, but he couldn't see her tears because of the rain.

'Well, as you can see, I'm still here, as hale and hearty as ever.'

'Yes, thank goodness!'

She hugged him even tighter and heard a couple of squeaks coming from inside his anorak. Glen laughed and extracted one of the dogs from the warmth of his body and handed it to her. Poor Candy looked like a drowned rat and as the thunder continued to roar overhead, she rolled big frightened eyes at Bernie.

'They ran off at the first crack of thunder,' Glen said. 'Fortunately, I saw them and went after them. Otherwise I might have been matchwood under that old tree.'

'Oh, Candy, my poor darling!'

Bernie hugged the dog to her. It nuzzled her neck, licking at the rain running down in rivulets.

'Apart from being very wet,' Glen shouted above the noise, 'I'd say we are all four of us OK, which is more than can be said for the cottage.'

Bernie, reminded of the near fatal disaster, turned to stare in horror at the ugly ruin the cottage had been reduced to. The stricken tree had sliced it in half, demolishing most of the roof. All the window panes had gone and there were branches sticking through the gaping windows like black skeleton arms waving about to attract attention. She gulped back a delayed panic attack and wiped away the mixture of rain and tears from her face.

'You'd better come back to the house,' she told him and, nodding his agreement, he followed her up the drive and into the dry warmth of the old manor house.

Once inside, Bernie led Glen up to the second floor where there was an en-suite bedroom and a wardrobe full of cousin George's clothes which she had considered too good to throw out, but had never got round to doing anything with them. Glen looked at the clothes askance and she quickly explained that George, bless his eccentric old heart, had been a bit of a recluse.

'He never married, then?' Glen wanted to know.

'No. He didn't really like people. He didn't much care for women in his life.'

'And he left you this house, you say?'

'Yes, the house and it's contents. He left a sum of money to my sister, but the house came to me.'

'Why was that, do you think?'

'Oh, I used to come here quite often with Belinda when Mum and Dad were having problems. Belinda hated it.'

'And you loved it?'

Bernie thought about that, then nodded slowly.

'Yes, I did. There's something about the house, despite all the big rooms and the old-fashioned furniture. It's a bit like having a big old, comfortable friend you can rely on to give you a cuddle when you need it, someone who'll keep you safe no matter what.'

Glen smiled and his eyes wrinkled with pleasurable understanding.

'It's the kind of home to raise a family in, the way they used to in the old days. I can see why you like it.'

Bernie's eyes dropped to the level of his anorak. She drew in a deep, throbbing sigh. He had hit the nail right on the head. That's exactly what she had always thought about the old place, what she had dreamed of doing since she was a little girl. In her mind she had planned family Christmases and seen herself with her husband and their children sitting around the Christmas tree, singing carols and eating turkey and stuffing and doing all the things she held dear at that time of year — things that had stopped with the death of her grandmother when she was a little girl.

'Yes, well, there's little hope of that,

I'm afraid,' she said and heaved a sigh. 'I've just put the house on the market.'

'You're selling it! But why, when you like it so much?'

'I don't want to sell it, but, well, I can't live on fresh air. Jobs are a bit thin on the ground and any kind of job I can do wouldn't pay for the necessary repairs and upkeep of a place like this. I think George thought I'd be married by the time he died, married with a bevy of children. Those impossible dreams again.'

She turned from him to hide a new spurt of tears to her eyes. There was a short silence, then she felt his light touch on her shoulder.

'Isn't there anyone in your life you could share that dream with, Bernie?'

She shook her head.

'No! And I don't want anybody. I can't trust anybody any more, not like that. When you've been hurt the way I was you get to thinking that every man must be the same, and they usually are, it seems to me.'

'Well, I beg to differ there, but then I'm a man and my bad experiences have all been with women. My wife wouldn't suffer children any more than she would suffer animals. As for my job, she couldn't stand the competition there either. It's not easy being the wife of a policeman. It took Paula six months to decide it simply wasn't for her. So you see, Bernie, you're not the only one in the world to know disappointment when it comes to personal relationships.'

'No, I daresay I'm not, but I'm not prepared to get hurt again.'

That was the moment when she felt his hands gripping her shoulders. He swung her around to face him with bruising force. When he spoke it was with fervour and she felt his warm breath wafting the stray hairs that had fallen across her forehead.

'Look at me, Bernie! Don't waste your life living on the memory of one hurtful experience. I did that for a while. I spent a long time feeling sorry for myself, then I took a really close look at all the things I held sacred, the things I valued most in life, and my job, the career I'd built just to please my father, didn't come all that high on my list. The sad thing is that at the end of the day my father isn't so proud of what I do, and my mother wouldn't care if I sold fruit at the local market as long as I'm happy and don't get into trouble.'

He paused for a few moments before carrying on.

'That's why I decided to take early retirement from the force and spend the rest of my life doing what I really want to do. I'm a pretty good artist, I get on well with most people, and I like teaching, not in a classroom, but out in the field. I want to open an arts centre, run some courses, that kind of thing. Of course, it might be nice to have someone at my side who could help with the organisation. Would you be interested, Bernie?'

Bernie opened her mouth to reply, not quite knowing what she was going to say. However, before she could form one single sentence, Glen had drawn her close to him and his lips were burning hers in a frenzy of passion that left her weak and trembling. His own voice, when he finally came up for breath, shook with emotion.

'I want you, Bernie. You know that, don't you?'

She pushed him away, shaking her head, not hiding the anger that burned in her eyes. He staggered backwards, blinking, not understanding.

'Oh, yes!' she cried out, despairingly. 'You've left me in no doubt about what that means. Well, you can just think again. You men all want just one thing.'

She saw his face crumple in surprise and disappointment. He started to say something, then anger flared in his eyes to match her own. He picked up his discarded anorak and marched out, following by a disconsolate looking Mop who went most of the way with backward glances. Candy followed them forlornly to the door, but did not venture over the step into the storm.

Bernie slammed the front door shut and made sure it was bolted. Then she stood with her back against the heavy oak panels and wept bitter tears of total frustration.

Why, she kept asking herself, over and over again? Why did he have to say those words, the very same words Philip had used on more than one occasion? They were words without meaning — I want, you know that I want you, don't you?

Of course he wanted her, but what did that kind of wanting have to do with love, of a permanent relationship?

Her father had also said those words to her mother. She had heard him, and shortly after, he had packed his bags and gone and he hadn't come back. He hadn't come back to see the woman he was supposed to want or the little girl he was supposed to love. Her father, too, could be called handsome. Women had been attracted to him. He had the same kind of charm as Philip and now

Glen. They were all out of the same mould.

It wasn't fair. Why couldn't she just find someone who was ordinary and wanted the things she wanted? The trouble was, the only thing she wanted at that precise moment was Glen Arden.

8

But, Bernie, you idiot, the man's an absolute gem! How could you turn him down?'

Bernie frowned into the phone as her sister lectured her on the subject of Glen Arden. Belinda had telephoned out of the blue simply to talk about him and Bernie wished she hadn't.

'Belinda, please, I'm just not in the mood to discuss him right now,' she said wearily.

'If I were you I'd burn all my boats and jump at the chance of being his woman, whatever the arrangement. In fact, if I weren't otherwise engaged, I'd steal him from you like a shot.'

'It would be just like old times,' Bernie mumbled into the phone caustically, but Belinda ignored the remark.

'Anyway, he says he's tried phoning you and you always hang up on him, and he's written and you don't reply. The man's besotted. Why on earth don't you give him a chance to prove his worth, Bernie?'

'He's too much like Philip, and Dad!'

'Rubbish! He's nothing like either of them and you know it. You're scared of getting hurt again, that's all. You're a coward, Bernie. Life's one big risk. Didn't you know that? You have to take the risks to get anything out of it, otherwise you vegetate, take root in your old armchair in front of the television, spending your life regretting all the things you haven't done.'

Bernie sighed.

'Anyway, how do you know all this about Glen? How do you know how he feels about me?' she asked her sister.

'He told me, darling. On a cold, wintry night he knocked on my door to tell me that my would-be aggressor had been apprehended and had confessed all. And can you believe this, it was my producer! She's been responsible for all the threatening e-mails I've been getting. I've no idea why. Jealousy, perhaps. Anyway, they've put a stop to her little game and I feel so much better. Of course, it does mean that I won't have the pleasure of seeing Glen again.'

'Oh? Well, I suppose he has other cases to solve.'

'He asked me to give you a message.'

'Wh . . . what did he say? Belinda?'

'Only that he's leaving tomorrow. He's been recalled to Scotland or something to finish his term of service. He says you have his number and all it takes is for you to phone him at midnight tonight if you ever want to see him again.'

'Oh, Belinda!'

Bernie felt her throat tighten. Her first gripped the telephone so tightly that her knuckles shone white.

'You will, of course!' Belinda said.

'I can't! If I call him it'll be like telling him he can have me on his terms. It's exactly how Philip used to keep me around. Always giving me promises he couldn't keep, or wouldn't keep.'

'Don't be ridiculous, Bernie! Do you want this man or don't you?'

'Yes, but, oh, Belinda, it'll just turn into another affair. I don't want that. I'm the old-fashioned type. I want marriage, a home, children.'

'Oh, poor you! Well, I have to say that the great Glen Arden doesn't exactly look that type. Handsome men never are, you know. They're too busy putting it about, but what an opportunity to miss.'

When midnight dragged itself around, Bernie was still awake and sitting by the telephone. Once, twice, three times, her fingers crept towards the instrument but she couldn't make herself punch in Glen's number. The chimes of the old grandfather clock in the hall rang out twelve. Bernie's stomach churned, her pulses raced, her heart tripped in its frantic haste, but she didn't ring.

At ten past midnight, with a heavy

heart full of regret, she dragged herself upstairs to bed. She lay for most of the night staring at the ceiling, willing Glen to ring her, but he didn't. There was nothing but the deafening silence of the empty house to keep her company. He had given her a second chance, a chance to change her mind. He wasn't the kind of man to swallow his pride and come back to her and she was sure he would never, ever beg.

* * *

It was three weeks to go before Christmas when the estate agent rang to say that he had found a buyer for the house. Bernie's heart leaped and sank at the same time. It was a blessing, she told herself, thinking of her impending overdraft at the bank. At the same time it meant she would lose the only thing she held dear — the house she loved so much.

'It's all a bit strange,' the agent said into her ear. 'The buyers are doing everything through their solicitor. The thing is, they want to move in immediately.'

'But they can't!' Bernie sang out.

'No, of course they can't, in the ordinary run of things,' the agent said and sounded hesitant. 'However, the solicitor's instructions were implicit. His clients will rent the house from you until such time as the sale becomes legal and binding. And, what's more . . .'

'Yes?'

Bernie held her breath.

'Well, they're insisting on everything being left as it is and sold with the house. Does that sound reasonable to you, Miss Brooks?'

'Reasonable! Of course, it doesn't! What do they mean by everything?'

'Oh, furniture, furnishings, nothing personal, of course!'

'And what am I supposed to do? Lock myself in the attic as part of the furnishings?'

'I do appreciate your difficulty, but

may I suggest a solution?'

'I'm listening.'

'These clients are prepared to pay a reasonable price for the house and its contents. Actually, they settled at a higher price than I ever expected to obtain for such a big, isolated house with so much needed in the way of renovation. If you'll pardon my candour, Miss Brooks, you'd be a fool not to accept.'

'But where am I to live in the meantime? It takes time to find a place.'

'Absolutely no problem, if you're agreeable.'

'Agreeable? To what?'

'I have a small studio flat available. It's furnished, so you don't have to rush out and buy furniture. It could see you over on a temporary basis until you find what you want. The thing is, Miss Brooks, with the sale of the house, and they've promised cash, you'll be able to pick and choose.'

The agent stopped abruptly and let his words sink in. Bernie thought about it and the realist in her told her it was too good a deal to pass up.

'Go ahead,' she said through gritted teeth, knowing it was the sensible decision, but she really had to say it quickly before she listened to her heart and changed her mind. 'Now, can you give me details of this flat you mentioned?'

The agent told her all about the studio apartment and they made arrangements to meet there the following day.

As she discovered, it was indeed small, but pleasant enough for a short stay until she found something more permanent. Rather than put things off, she set to immediately and gathered together her more personal belongings and left cousin George's house not daring to give a backward glance. There was a huge lump in her throat that refused to go away until she had had a good, long cry.

The week before Christmas, Bernie found a job as a temporary secretary at the local paint factory. The pay was poor, the working conditions appalling, but it was a start and better than nothing. And, of course, she already had the rent for the house in her bank account, one month in advance.

On Christmas Eve, she went shopping. Belinda had actually invited her to spend Christmas Day with her and Edward, so she treated herself to a nice new outfit. So what if Belinda spent most of the time criticising her and Edward fell asleep over his plum pudding, it was infinitely better than spending Christmas alone.

She bought presents for everybody, not that it came to any grand number. She purchased an extravagant piece of jewellery for her mother, which she probably wouldn't like, an Indian silk shawl for Belinda in the gaudy colours she preferred, expensive cologne for Edward, a set of comedy videos for her best friend whom she hardly ever saw any more, and a box of cigars for her father which she would post to him.

She would receive a brief note of thanks and a cheque in return.

She tried not to think of Glen Arden, but she failed miserably. Of course she was curious to know what he was doing, especially at this time of year. He was probably celebrating his retirement, and, more than likely, he had some attractive blond or brunette in tow. He wasn't the kind of man to be without female company for any length of time.

The thought of Glen having girl-friends left, right and centre, disturbed her. It was stupid, she knew, since she herself had had the opportunity of a cosy relationship with him and she had turned her back on it. Not a moment went by that she didn't regret her decision. Maybe, after all, it was better to have loved a little and be loved, than never to have loved at all.

She had just staggered back from the shops, laden with parcels, when the doorbell rang. She groaned and looked longingly at the cup of much-needed tea she had poured. On opening the door she was met by an immense red poinsettia and a face hiding behind it loudly and tunelessly singing, 'While shepherds washed their socks by night!'

Oh, no! It was the young man from the next-door flat! He had gone out of his way to make her feel welcome and wanted, especially wanted. He was the type who didn't easily take the hint, but kept on trying anyway.

'Oh, Rob, you fool! Do shut up!'

This was virtually an invitation to make him go on singing in an even louder voice until she was forced to invite him in rather than face the wrath of the other residents. His flyaway hair was down to his shoulders in unfashionable disarray; his once cream sweater was stretched and grubby; his brown cords creased and baggy. On his feet he wore a pair of shabby, plastic trainers.

'Hi, there, beautiful! Merry Christmas! Wanna make music with me tonight?'

He pushed the enormous plant into her arms and marched into the flat, looking left and right as if inspecting the premises. It was the first time she had allowed him inside. She wished she had been more adamant this time. He was hardly her type, even if she had been looking, which she wasn't.

'Thank you for the poinsettia,' she said, putting the plant carefully on the side table in the hall and following him into the bed-sit living-room. 'But you really shouldn't have.'

'Hey, you're a bit cramped for space in here, aren't you?'

He was eyeing the pull-down bed that she hadn't had time to make properly before hurrying off to work that morning.

'Cosy, though, eh?'

'It's just a temporary base,' she informed him quickly, 'until I find a house. I don't like flats.'

'You doing anything tonight? I thought maybe you'd like to come out for a meal and then wait for Santa Claus with me. You never know what kind of treats he might bring you. I've had a word in his ear. We're on first name terms, and he tells me that you're one mighty lonely lady.'

'On the contrary!' Bernie answered him with words that were tinged with anger. 'I choose to live on my own because I'm tired of people . . . men in particular . . . taking advantage of me.'

He grinned inanely at her. She simmered inside, but kept her emotions off the boil. It wasn't worth the effort, not for such an idiot as Rob. He had already proved to her that he was thick-skinned, which was probably why he was still single and still searching.

'Hey, Bernie, I'd give anything for you to take advantage of me,' Rob said, blinking at her with his wide and innocent eyes. 'Mmmm! You always smell so good!'

'Which is more than I can say for you, young man!'

He was probably about the same age as she was, but she always felt she was years older.

'Don't you ever take a bath? Wash your clothes?'

'It's not that bad, is it?'

'Believe me!'

'But other than that, you like me, don't you?'

'That depends, Rob. Look, you're basically a nice person. You're jolly and funny, in your way. I think you mean well and I've been grateful for the welcome you've given me since I arrived.'

'So? What's the problem?'

'I really don't fancy you,' Bernie blurted out, 'to put it honestly and bluntly.'

'Oh! OK!'

Rob held up both hands, palms facing her.

'I get the message. How about a kiss and a cuddle under the mistletoe?'

He immediately produced a scanty piece of crushed mistletoe from his pocket and held it over his head.

'No?' he said, feigning great dismay and disappointment.

'No!'

'Anything at all?'

'A cup of tea perhaps?'

'Sold! For that you can keep the poinsettia.'

Bernie grinned and felt a twinge of sympathy for her neighbour. He was hopeless and harmless, she was sure, but she didn't want to give him too much encouragement. The last thing she wanted was to have to deal with a lovelorn young man on her doorstep.

'What are you doing tomorrow?' she asked tentatively, thinking of the small turkey nestling among the rest of her shopping, which would be embarrassingly large for one.

He shrugged his shoulders and pulled a face.

'I'll probably go down to the pub and sink a few pints, drown a few sorrows with the lads.'

They both jumped as someone leaned heavily on the doorbell.

'Oh, dear! Not another visitor, surely!' Bernie groaned and on her way to answer the summons she called out over her shoulder for Rob to pour out two cups of tea and find some biscuits to go with it.

There was a uniformed messenger standing in the lobby with creaking black leathers splattered with raindrops.

'Miss Bernadette Brooks?' he asked in a voice muffled because of the huge, space-age crash helmet he was wearing.

She nodded and looked at him expectantly.

'Message for you.'

Bernie took the small, flat envelope he handed out to her and stared at it curiously. Then she slid her thumb under the flap and prised it open.

My dear Miss Brooks, she read. *Apologies for the late notice of this invitation, but would you care to join us for Christmas lunch? It would give us much pleasure and, hopefully, do the same for you. Please come at midday. With thanks and very best wishes.* It was signed, enigmatically, *The new occupiers of your delightful home*.

She drew in a deep breath and started to ask the messenger the name of the sender of the invitation, but he was already gone, his footsteps echoing on the marble slabs of the ground floor. Seconds later, the outer doors slammed shut behind him. Too late to ask him to take back a reply. She looked again at the note. There wasn't a name. Would they be disappointed if she didn't turn up tomorrow? They didn't even know her! Besides, they should at least have given her some notice and provided her with a current phone number to ring.

She knew for a fact that the telephone had been changed and the number with it. The estate agent had informed her that the new owners preferred to be ex-directory. Well, she couldn't blame them for that.

'What is it? You've not won the lottery, have you? No? Shame.'

Rob was standing in the door of the living-room, cup of tea in his hand, eyeing Candy who was eyeing him with disapproval and had a low growl gurgling in her throat.

'What's up with him?'

'It's her, and don't take any notice of her. She's going through a difficult time. She's pregnant.'

Even as she said the words, Bernie felt her heart tweak uncomfortably.

'Saucy little thing!'

Rob grinned and wagged a finger at the little Yorkie who looked at him plaintively.

'It wasn't that big Doberman on the ground floor, was it?'

'Don't be ridiculous, Rob.'

Bernie tried to smile, but it went all wobbly as she thought of tangle-haired Mop and his immaculate owner.

'What about having Christmas dinner together then? I could stretch to a bottle of something white and sparkling if you like.'

Bernie smiled gratefully and shook her head.

'Sorry, Rob, but I'm spending Christmas with some friends.'

When Rob had gone, Bernie phoned

her sister. Maybe it was all in her imagination, but she thought there was some relief in Belinda's voice when she heard that Bernie had decided not to spend Christmas with her after all.

9

Bernie sorted out her shopping, wrapped the few presents she had and put the turkey in the freezer. She had been apprehensive at the thought of spending Christmas Day with Belinda and Edward, but now things looked a bit more cheerful.

The people, whoever they were, who now lived in her old home, were obviously very friendly, or they would never have thought to invite her on such a special, family occasion, or were they already feeling rather isolated, rattling around in that great mausoleum which would surely intimidate most people?

'Oh, goodness!'

Bernie's hands flew to her face as she realised she didn't have a gift to take to them. Then her eyes alighted on the poinsettia. It was very big and certainly beautiful, but she wasn't much good at looking after house plants. Besides, it was so enormous it dominated the flat. Shame to let it go to waste when it could be appreciated more fully per- haps by the people buying her house.

'Right!' she went on, talking softly to herself as she searched among a box of her personal effects which hadn't yet been unpacked. 'There are some festive bows and ribbons in here somewhere. As long as Rob doesn't see me go tomorrow, it won't upset him that I'm giving his plant to somebody else. Ah, there!'

She wrapped a bright green ribbon around the terracotta pot and stuck on a white satin rosette that was decorated with tiny sprigs of holly. Now she felt better. She couldn't possibly have turned up at the house empty-handed.

After a light meal, Bernie was washing up in the tiny kitchen corner when something made her glance out of the window. Fluffy white flakes of snow were falling from a dark sky. She sighed. Well, at least she was having part of her Christmas dream come true, the dream where she is happily married to a man who looked so much like Glen Arden it was depressing, a dream where they lived in a big house in the country and were surrounded by their children and a loving family all having a jolly time around the Christmas tree, eating turkey and mince pies and singing and laughing together.

Well, Bernie, she thought, you'll just have to settle for a white Christmas. Anything else will be a bonus.

She heard Rob coming in very late and very drunk well after midnight. He banged on her door and wished her a rather slurred Merry Christmas, then all was silent. It was doubtful he would be awake before midday, by which time she would already be at cousin George's house, meeting new friends.

Christmas morning was sunny and bright. The roofs and the streets below them were thick with crisp white snow. Even the air had a festive feel about it, though Bernie was still experiencing a sad ache deep within her rib cage. She ought to have been used to it by now, having spent so many miserable Christmases alone, away from her parents, away from Philip. At least this time she would have some company, even if they were some old, decrepit couple of eccentrics.

Bernie wore the new outfit she had bought and hoped it wouldn't look too dressy. She'd chosen midnight blue velour pants with a satiny sheen and a matching tunic in heavy silk patterned with self-coloured flock roses. She was pleased to see that the colour suited her and the style gave her quite a sylph-like appearance. She added silver hoop earrings and a heavy silver locket on a chain. A light touch of make-up and she was ready.

Her small car took a bit of coaxing to start, but eventually she set off, driving carefully on the dangerously slushy roads, with Candy beside her. The town was quiet, though there were some people out and about, mainly families, she noticed. In the park children were building snowmen and having snowball fights. A white Christmas was rare these days. It made Bernie feel as if she were slipping back in time to the days when she was a happy child and all was right with her world and her future was not an issue of the day, good, bad or indifferent.

As she passed the church in the square the sound of Christmas carols wafted out, voices raised in unison. She wasn't overly religious, but how she had loved going to church on Christmas morning. That, too, had slipped into the forgotten and discarded past. Around the next corner the brass band of the Salvation Army was blasting out a carol to the accompaniment of a booming base drum and jingling tambourines. As they played and sang, clouds of vapour escaped into the iced air. Bernie hummed along with them as she drove on, getting all choked up on a lump of sentimentality.

She arrived at cousin George's house almost before she realised it. She parked the car on the road outside, wanting to walk up the drive, which, she noticed, had already been cleared of snow and grit put down. Tiny fairy lights were strewn in the trees and across the front of the house. They were lit up, in all their colourful splendour. On the front door, which was partially open, was hung a large wreath of holly with clusters of blood red berries.

These people, she thought as she rang the bell, really knew how to celebrate Christmas.

Since there was no answer to her ringing, she knocked sharply with her knuckles, waited some seconds, then stepped inside.

'Hello!' she called out, noticing that the hall was also decorated tastefully in the festive spirit.

Some Christmas music was playing softly somewhere. The smell of hot, spiced wine drifted out of the kitchen, mingled with roasting turkey and sage and onion stuffing.

'Hello! Is anybody there?' she repeated.

'In here!'

A voice summoned her from the lounge, the larger of the two reception rooms. Something in the familiar tone of the deep, male voice made her hesitate and swallow back a sudden rise of panicking butterflies which had exploded in her stomach.

'Come in!'

She closed the front door behind her and walked with uncertain steps across the hall and into the lounge. He was standing at the fireplace, facing a roaring fire, immensely tall, broad shouldered with long, muscular legs. He turned and she saw the handsome face and the piercing blue eyes that had haunted her dreams for the past few weeks. She felt as if she had known that face all her life, and the man it belonged to.

'Glen!'

'Hello, Bernie,' he said as he came

forward, taking the trembling poinsettia out of her hands and putting it to one side. 'Merry Christmas. Thank you for coming.'

'But . . . why didn't you say it was you? I mean . . . I . . . '

She really didn't know what she meant. She could only stand there, blinking up at him in astonishment, her knees quaking.

'I didn't dare let you know it was me. You might not have come and all this . . . '

His eyes made a general sweep of the room.

'All this would have been in vain. How are you? You look wonderful.'

'I . . . I'm fine, but Candy's not very happy. She's to be having puppies.' His eyes twinkled at her.

'I wondered if that might happen. Where is she? Didn't you bring her with you?'

'I couldn't leave her on her own on Christmas Day. She's in the car.'

'Mop will be ecstatic to find his true

love again. He's been miserable and not the easiest of dogs to live with, and that makes two of us.'

Bernie took a deep breath.

'Greg, I don't understand. I thought you'd gone back to Scotland.'

Her voice sounded loud yet muffled in her ears. If she didn't get to sit down shortly, she thought, she would surely faint with the shock of seeing him again so unexpectedly.

'I did go back home to Scotland,' he said, leading her to a chair and gently pushing her into it. 'I had a case to tie up. Nothing too difficult. After speaking with your sister . . . '

'Belinda! What did she say to you?'

'Nothing that I didn't already know, but it was nice to have it confirmed.'

'And that was?'

'That you were . . . are in love with me.'

'How dare she interfere!'

'Well, somebody had to speak out on your behalf, since you were content to bury your feelings because you were too scared to get hurt a second time. I'm not counting your father. Philip may or may not have been like him, but I assure you, Bernie, that I was not cast in the same mould and I intend to prove that to you, today, and for the rest of my life, if you'll just let me, please.'

Her heart stumbled, but she frowned at him angrily just the same.

'You've started off rather on the wrong foot, don't you think? I've a good mind to put a stop to the sale of this house.'

'Oh, be quiet, woman and just listen to me!'

He spoke sharply, and she suddenly closed her mouth, but his eyes were still smiling.

'I think it's time you met the real new owners of your cousin George's house.'

'It's not you then?' she asked breathlessly.

'Not entirely,' he said, shaking his head and taking up a folded legal document from the coffee table. 'I had this drawn up. It's legal and binding, once it's signed. However, if you don't like what you see there you can throw it in the fire and we'll call the deal off. But I don't want you to do that until this day is over. Have I your promise?'

His eyes said it was the least she could do. Her heart rushed to agree, while her head firmly told her to tread warily. Her throat had become as dry as a desert. She swallowed with difficulty and nodded.

'Yes, all right.'

Glen gave her the document. She didn't have to read through all the legal jargon to know what it was he had done. She looked up from the stiff solicitor's parchment, her mouth opening and closing, her brain in a knot, her senses reeling.

'What does this all mean?'

'It means, Bernie, my sweet, that you and I are the joint owners of this incredible mausoleum.'

'I don't understand, Glen. That's not my name there . . . it's . . . '

'Mr Glen Arden and Mrs Bernadette Arden, which, my darling Bernie, is what you will be, if you marry me.'

'Marry you!'

Her words sounded feeble, hardly above a whisper. Everything was rushing in on her, threatening to suffocate her.

'Well, among other things it would make an honest woman of Candy. She and Mop make a great couple, don't you think?'

When she just stood there, biting on her lips and shaking her head, he threw back his head impatiently.

'Bernie, what do I have to do? Get down on my knees and plead?'

He fell on to his knees before her, his strong hands gripping her wrists.

'Bernie, we want the same things, you and I. We want the security of a happy marriage, children, a home we can be proud of but comfortable in. We want to be part of a family that loves one another. High-powered careers and mistresses are out, and whether you believe me or not they were never my cup of tea anyway.'

'I don't know what to say, what to think even.'

Bernie's heart was beating so madly she thought it might burst. Her eyes were filling with tears. She couldn't help it. It was all too much for her to take in, too big for her to cope with.

She gave a loud gulp as Glen's hands now framed her face, his thumbs caressing her cheeks. His eyes, more intensely blue than ever before, searched for the answer he was willing her to give him. He looked so serious, so intense, and so much in love.

'Well, Bernie?'

His voice cracked on her name, then he cleared his throat and went on.

'I once told you that I wasn't known for doing rash things. Well, that's true, but the first time I saw you, long before we met, I had the feeling that you and I could be so right for one another, only at the time I thought you were that infernal sister of yours and married to boot. You've no idea how relieved I was to discover just how wrong I was.'

Still she held back, terrified of committing herself, not daring to trust him, yet knowing that she wanted to, knowing that she was being as silly as Belinda had said she was. Glen stood up and pulled her to him. His arms slid around her, encircling her in a tender embrace that held no threat for her.

'No more words now,' he whispered hoarsely as his lips found hers.

She sagged helplessly against him, felt the solid beat of his heart accelerating against her. As his face came close, her lips parted to receive his kiss. There was no going back now. She knew that she wanted him every bit as passionately as he so obviously wanted her. Her eyes opened, gazed up at him as he pulled away from her and she knew from his expression that he was finding it difficult.

'That was the sweetest kiss I've ever tasted,' he said.

'For me, too, Glen.'

'I love you, Bernie,' Glen croaked, his eyes reflecting the bittersweet pain she herself was experiencing. 'Do you love me? Will you marry me, please?'

Words refused to come. She bit her lower lip and nodded once, a tiny dip of the head, then she found her voice again, though her throat was so tight with pent-up emotion it was almost impossible to speak coherently.

'Yes, Glen, I do love you. I've been trying to fight it, but I can't any more. I was such a fool to send you away. And, yes, I think maybe I will marry you.'

'I want you all to myself, Bernie, but there isn't time, my love.'

He gave her a rueful smile.

'It's Christmas Day and in about half an hour you're going to meet my family who are all invited here for Christmas lunch.'

'Oh! Oh, goodness!'

Bernie's hand went up to her hair which had become disarrayed, and her fingers touched her lips where there had once been a careful application of lipstick.

'You still look wonderful to me, but go and see to the damage I've caused, then come and help me finish off trimming this tree. The turkey and the plum pudding are already cooking merrily. Everything else is prepared and ready to go when it's time.'

'You really can cook!' Bernie exclaimed on her way to the hall.

'Of course I can. My mother believes in everybody being equal, so she gave us all lessons in how to survive in the kitchen, even the boys. Go on, I know how you women like to look your best when meeting other women for the first time. You go and patch your face up and I'll fetch Candy.'

Bernie rushed upstairs, tamed her hair and replaced her lipstick. Her reflection stared back at her in disbelief — cheeks aflame, a mouth still trembling from the magic of Glen's kisses, eyes so bright they would undoubtedly give the game away. If she hung out banners and rang church bells, the signs could not be any clearer. She was in love, head over heels in love, and, she decided, it really was for the very first time, and the last, she was sure.

THE END

We do hope that you have enjoyed reading this large print book.

Did you know that all of our titles are available for purchase?

We publish a wide range of high quality large print books including:
Romances, Mysteries, Classics
General Fiction
Non Fiction and Westerns

Special interest titles available in large print are:
The Little Oxford Dictionary
Music Book, Song Book
Hymn Book, Service Book

Also available from us courtesy of Oxford University Press:
Young Readers' Dictionary
(large print edition)
Young Readers' Thesaurus
(large print edition)

For further information or a free brochure, please contact us at:
Ulverscroft Large Print Books Ltd.,
The Green, Bradgate Road, Anstey,
Leicester, LE7 7FU, England.
Tel: (00 44) **0116 236 4325**
Fax: (00 44) **0116 234 0205**

CONVALESCENT HEART

Lynne Collins

They called Romily the Snow Queen, but once she had been all fire and passion, kindled into loving by a man's kiss and sure it would last a lifetime. She still believed it would, for her. It had lasted only a few months for the man who had stormed into her heart. After Greg, how could she trust any man again? So was it likely that surgeon Jake Conway could pierce the icy armour that the lovely ward sister had wrapped about her emotions?

TOO MANY LOVES

Juliet Gray

Justin Caldwell, a famous personality of stage and screen, was blessed with good looks and charm that few women could resist. Stacy was a newcomer to England and she was not impressed by the handsome stranger; she thought him arrogant, ill-mannered and detestable. By the time that Justin desired to begin again on a new footing it was much too late to redeem himself in her eyes, for there had been too many loves in his life.

MYSTERY AT MELBECK

Gillian Kaye

Meg Bowering goes to Melbeck House in the Yorkshire Dales to nurse the rich, elderly Mrs Peacock. She likes her patient and is immediately attracted to Mrs Peacock's nephew and heir, Geoffrey, who farms nearby. But Geoffrey is a gambling man and Meg could never have foreseen the dreadful chain of events which follow. Throughout her ordeal, she is helped by the local vicar, Andrew Sheratt, and she soon discovers where her heart really lies.

HEART UNDER SIEGE

Joy St Clair

Gemma had no interest in men
— which was how she had acquired
the job of companion/secretary to
Mrs Prescott in Kentucky. The old
lady had stipulated that she wanted
someone who would not want to
rush off and get married. But why
was the infuriating Shade Lambert
so sceptical about it? Gemma was
determined to prove to him that she
meant what she said about remain-
ing single — but all she proved was
that she was far from immune to his
devastating attraction!

HOME IS WHERE THE HEART IS

Mavis Thomas

Venetia had loved her husband dearly. Now she and their small daughter were living alone in a beautiful, empty home. Seeking fresh horizons in a Northern seaside town, Venetia finds deep interest in work with a Day Centre for the Elderly — and two very different men. If ever she could rediscover love, would Terry bring it with his caring, healing laughter? Or would it be Jay, the once well-known singer now at the final crossroads of his troubled career?

THE ELUSIVE DOCTOR

Claire Vernon

Wearing spectacles to make herself appear more dignified, twenty-year-old Candy gained the longed-for post as secretary to the two principals of a school in the African mountains. She was often overworked, sometimes shocked, occasionally unhappy. But all through her days at the school there ran a single thread, which bound her to the one person with whom she felt most at ease, the man who finally said unforgivable, hurtful things — the man she could not forget.